Tamonten Tusks

FOUR HEAVENLY KINGS

IVAN WAIN

First edition ISBN: 978-1-8382207-3-0
Editing by Lesley Jones
Illustration by Affendy Ilias

This book is dedicated to my parents Marie and Reg, my wife's father Tony and my brother-in-law Allan Jones. We miss them all and believe they would have been hugely supportive.

'I will show you something different from either
Your shadow at morning striding behind you
Or your shadow at evening rising to meet you;
I will show you fear in a handful of dust.'
-*T.S. Eliot, "The Waste Land"*

TAMONTEN TUSKS

Tam on Ten Tusks

Tamonten are the four Heavenly Kings.

This story is a tribute to all the animal conservationists in the world who care about protecting endangered species and holding on to our priceless neighbours, never permitting their extinction.

The four main characters – Kintaro, Yuki-Onna (Yuki), Nakano (Takeko) and Issun Boshi (Bosh) – are very special elephants who have been granted specific powers by Narok, one of the gods of the savanna.

The inspiration for the main characters was taken from Japanese folklore and fairy tales to inspire the reader to engage with the characters' personalities.

The story tells of how the Tamonten Tusks inherited their powers, how they came together, and the many adventures they experience in their quest to highlight the plight of endangered animals. It exposes the illegal trade of ivory and the impact of man's greed for more and more land.

1

Issun Boshi

One sun boy

M arie was a mature cow elephant and had come to terms with the fact that this may be her last pregnancy. She had been in labour for days but felt that this evening would see the arrival of her fifth calf.

The full term had been different this time, which she found difficult to explain to her friends and midwives, Cody, Priya, and Darsha, who were in close attendance.

'Doesn't feel the same as last time,' she said.

Darsha was quick to respond. 'Don't be silly, Marie, you look the picture of health and it's going to be fine.'

Priya and Cody were also quick to dismiss her concerns and soon got her focusing on the exciting event.

The friends slowly manoeuvred her to an appropriate location in undisturbed long grasses and among a plethora of shrubs. Perfect for the happy occasion.

It was still very warm in the evening after the searing heat of the day, which added to Marie's discomfort. However, the reassuring sounds of the cicadas and chirping crickets made her feel at ease, although she was disturbed by the annoying laughter of hyenas in the vicinity calling to their cubs.

Marie paced up and down as the labour pains intensified.

The birth was close, and the others watched her with the same maternal instinct Marie had afforded them when they had given birth to their calves in the past.

Finally, with one last momentous outburst and crowning push, she delivered her amniotic sac, which dropped some three feet to its dusty destination. Amid the euphoria and relief, Marie's exhausted frame dropped to its knees then slumped onto the ground, motionless.

'What's wrong with her?' said Pryia.

'Oh my god, she's been shot,' said Cody.

As Marie slumped to the ground, narrowly missing her sac, Pryia noticed a dart in Marie's back leg. 'It's poachers,' she cried, and instinctively charged in a random direction, as did Darsha in the opposite direction, covering all angles.

Cody stayed and attended to Marie.

When the two brave friends returned, having frightened off the poachers, they found Cody sobbing uncontrollably and realised it was too late. Marie had succumbed to the deadly toxins in the dart and all signs of life had left her.

The three friends rocked their heads from side to side in overwhelming grief. They towered over Marie's lifeless frame as if to protect her from any further horrors.

'I can't believe she's gone,' said Pryia, unable to hold back tears.

'There's nothing more we can do for her, but what about the calf? Is it still alive?' asked Darsha. She moved towards the birth sac, blew on it, and gently nudged it with her trunk. Immediately, the amniotic sac burst, and Darsha started to remove the membrane revealing an empty, barren sac, which should have contained the baby elephant.

'Where is the calf?' asked Priya. 'Maybe it got scared and ran off?'

'Don't be such an idiot,' said Darsha. 'We have only just opened the sac up and calves cannot stand for a least an hour, let alone run into the bush.'

'Wait a minute,' said Cody, 'something is wriggling about within the fluid. Oh, to the gods of the savanna, it's alive.'

'What's alive? I can't see anything,' said Priya.

'It's unbelievable, incredible. Look closely – it's tiny, it can't be much bigger than a dung beetle in length. But it looks perfectly formed,' said Darsha.

'It's a freak, that's what it is,' said Pryia. 'What shall we do with it? There's no way it can survive.'

'Let me put my foot on it and put it out of its misery,' said Cody. 'It's for the best.'

'How could you, Cody? It's Marie's child,' said Darsha.

'Poor Marie is not with us anymore. Who is going to look after it, if it does survive?'

'I think Cody's right,' said Pryia, and it was clear that two out of the three friends had voted to put an end to the hapless newborn.

'Back off, ladies,' shouted Darsha.

Just as she was escorting the two ladies away, a martial eagle swooped down and gathered the infant in his talons and climbed into the night sky. The three elephants were completely bewildered at the sight of the eagle but quickly concluded that it would probably return to its nest and feed it to one of its eaglets.

The eagle spoke as it climbed. 'Do not worry, ladies, no harm will come to him. This is a very special elephant and, in time, you will hear about his adventures and they will become legendary.'

He climbed higher and higher and out of sight.

**

Narok, the all-seeing eagle, cherished the powers and great responsibility given to him by the Heavenly Kings. 'Don't worry, little one, you will be safe now. My name is Narok and the gods have great plans for you and, when your time comes, you will be revered by many and play a crucial role in the survival of our kingdom.'

After only a short flight, they landed on a nest in a thorny acacia tree, perched a safe height above the ground. The nest was made of twigs and stretched about the width of the tree's foliage in diameter.

Green leaves lined the infant's new home, which made it perfectly comfortable, and there was a plentiful supply of food – not that the new arrival needed much.

'What's happening to me?' said the infant. 'Where is my mother?'

'I am sorry to have to tell you, little one, that your mother was killed by poachers shortly after giving birth to you,' Narok explained. 'But fear not, I am here to take good care of you.'

'Why am I so small? Shouldn't I be bigger than this?'

'You are just perfect,' insisted Narok, 'and you will eventually experience a gift the gods have bestowed upon you, which will more than compensate for your diminutive size. The gift will become apparent when the time is right. I will soon place you with some friends of mine, who will care for and educate you. You are very special little one – never forget that.'

***

A week later, Narok explained that the time had come for the infant to meet his new foster parents. 'They are good people. Try not to worry – I will never be far away. They don't call me the all-seeing eagle for nothing,' said Narok.

He placed the infant on the back of his neck and leapt into the air.

The flight lasted for a couple of hours, before they came into land at the foot of a huge baobab tree almost twice the size of Narok's tree, and wide enough to fit two fully grown bull elephants inside, trunk to tail.

'This is your new home, little one. It's known as the tree of life and its inhabitants will take care of you until you reach an age where you can embark on the next chapter of your life,' said Narok.

The eagle landed softly and a family of chacma baboons emerged from the hollow tree to greet the new arrivals.

'Welcome, Narok,' said Swiss, the head of the troop, who was accompanied by Perrin, her partner, 'welcome to our humble abode.'

The infant looked on in amazement at the sight of about twenty terrifying-looking animals of all ages. Numerous babies clung to their mother's sides and juveniles bounced about excitedly. Slower, more mature baboons edged forward to take a closer look.

'And who is this little chappie?' said Perrin.

'I had hoped that you would give him a name, one fitting for someone so special,' said Narok.

'We will call him Issun,' pronounced Swiss, 'He reminds of an ancient tale of a tiny one inch child and that one sun is the Japanese word for inch and Boshi meaning boy, Issun Boshi.'

'Perfect,' said Narok. 'You know what to do. Teach him your values, equip him with the necessary skills, and educate him like one of your own. When the time is right, he will need to leave you and his quest will begin.'

Narok said his farewells and headed off into the afternoon sun.

'Let us show you around and introduce you to our troop,' said Swiss.

Perrin carefully picked up Issun Boshi and took him

inside the great hollow tree, closely followed by Swiss.

'Wow,' said Issun, amazed at the size of the tree.

'This tree has everything we need – fire-resistant shelter, a fruit called monkey bread, and water within its trunk,' said Perrin.

Swiss turned to face Issun.

'Now, let's get you settled in, Bosh – can we call you Bosh?' She said.

'That's fine with me. I haven't had the chance to get used to a name yet,' Issun replied.

Swiss and Perrin were thrilled at the prospect of being foster parents to Issun Boshi, or Bosh, because they hadn't been blessed with children of their own.

They relished the challenge of integrating him into their community and the teaching process started almost immediately.

***

The first five years of Bosh's life elapsed and the tiny elephant did not grow at all. He stayed the same size as he was the day Narok had placed him in their care.

At the age of ten, Bosh was becoming more and more inquisitive about everything in the baboon world. He now understood their language and was accepted, educated, protected, and adored by everyone in the troop.

What was most fascinating and interesting to Bosh was watching his parents exercise daily, using what looked like bamboo staffs.

'What are you doing?' Bosh asked Swiss.

'It's called tahtib, which originated in north-west Africa. The discipline helps to cultivate a vigorous spirit and mould the mind and body,' she said.

'But aren't you trying to hurt each other?' Bosh replied.

'It is a form of self-defence, yes, but we are not trying to hurt each other. It teaches us discipline, courtesy, and honour,' said Perrin.

Bosh became fascinated with watching his parents train and never missed a session. One day, to his surprise, they presented him with an ivory sewing needle, which looked like a scaled-down bamboo staff.

'Please accept this gift, Bosh. It was presented to us by an elephant friend of ours, who had damaged one of his tusks. He gave us this tiny sliver of ivory and my grandfather carved it into a needle. We have used for many years. This needle will be your asaya,' said Swiss.

Bosh was overjoyed and thanked his parents, then immediately got to work mimicking their moves as they trained.

'He's picking up the technique quickly,' Perrin said to Swiss.

'Yes, he has real talent, but we need to get him a sparring partner so he can train properly,' she replied.

On the day of Issun Boshi's eighteenth birthday, Swiss and Perrin summoned Bosh from his daily chore of plucking wax from baby baboons' ears.

'We have a very special present, or should we say a special someone for you, Bosh,' they said simultaneously.

'Who is that?' Bosh asked excitedly.

'Meet Arthur.' From behind her back, Swiss produced a tiny African pygmy mouse, not yet fully grown but the exact size of Issun Boshi.

Bosh could not contain his excitement and was even more astonished when the tiny rodent spoke to him.

'Hello, Bosh. I've heard a lot about you and I have to say that I didn't believe it when they said you were an elephant, the same size as me!'

'Pleased to meet you, Arthur and good things come in small packages, or so Perrin keeps telling me,' said Bosh.

The two became inseparable friends and developed a great passion for the sport of tahtib, mimicking the baboons and sparring from dawn until dusk. It was not long before they were both highly skilled in the art, even adding their own slant on technique. Additional self-defence moves, which both Swiss and Perrin were keen to adopt themselves.

Bosh joked that he needed to develop his skills even more because Arthur had grown to full size, which was twice Bosh's height!

Life with Arthur and the troop could not have been better, until the day when the peace and tranquillity was replaced by a living nightmare.

***

It was late afternoon in the savanna. The young were playing outside and the elders were preparing food for the troop that evening. Swiss and Perrin had left the baobab in search of cork bark, which they needed to carry out repairs.

Bosh and Arthur were inside the tree practising when they heard several agitated screams outside.

'What's happening?' said Bosh,

'I don't know, Arthur replied, 'quick let's get outside and see.'

The troop was under attack and the two friends could see that it was hyenas.

The shrieking and growling got closer and closer, and sent panic throughout the homestead. The adult male and female baboons gathered in a defensive formation, monitoring the pack mentality of the hyenas patrolling the circumference of the tree.

One by one, the hyenas tormented the troop, frequently lunging forward in the hope of drawing a monkey out, yet still the troop held firm until one cunning hyena saw its opportunity and pounced on an unsuspecting chacma infant, dragging it into the bush.

Bosh witnessed a horror he had never encountered before and suddenly felt emotions he had not experienced either. The gravity of what he had just seen filled him with both fright and anger. He leapt out of the tree and landed on the ground, using his ivory needle to steady his landing.

To the astonishment of everyone, including himself, Issun started to grow in size, eventually reaching the height of a fully grown African elephant, brandishing a life-size ivory asaya staff.

His anger took precedence over his sudden transformation and he turned to instinctive combat mode. Standing upright and very tall, he charged at the oncoming hyenas, wielding his needle with precision and administering fatal blow after blow upon the wild dogs, killing four or five instantly.

The remaining hyenas fled in despair at the sight of such a vengeful adversary as Issun Boshi. Their leader, however, remained at a safe distance, taking in the events and keeping out of harm's way, as her pack retreated to join her.

***

Swiss and Perrin raced back on hearing the distress calls and commotion from afar. They were just in time to witness the transformation of their adopted son and his devastating impact on the troop's assailants.

'So now we know, Bosh,' said Swiss, 'this is the special power that Narok had predicted would emerge.'

'What just happened to me?' said Bosh.

'You saved us, Bosh, and we cannot thank you enough for your bravery. Our casualties may have been much worse,' said Perrin.

Moments later, Issun Boshi reverted to his previous size, and, once he was back to normal, Arthur hugged him in appreciation of his friend's bravery.

Perrin picked up Bosh in his hand. 'Remember this day, Bosh, and reflect on what just happened. Narok has given you a gift, but it appears to be a power either sparked by emotion or, as Arthur pointed out, the slamming of your needle against the ground. Whatever it is, the transformation seems to be short-lived, so use your new-found power wisely.'

Swiss stood at her partner's side. 'Bosh, it is with huge regret and a heavy heart that we are duty-bound to tell you your time with us has come to an end. We have enjoyed having you with us, but you must leave now, to follow the path the gods have set out for you.'

'But I don't want to leave you, I'm not ready to leave,' Bosh replied.

'Don't worry, little one,' said Perrin, 'I'm sure we will see you again. Narok will see to that.'

Arthur made his way towards his friend and hugged him. 'Take good care, Bosh, and remember that if you ever need me, I will be there for you.'

'I'm going to miss all of you so much, but especially you, Arthur,' said Bosh.

At that moment and, as Issun Boshi had experienced before, Narok swooped down and carefully collected him in his talons and whisked him away to start the next chapter of his amazing life.

2

Kintaro

Golden boy and child of superhuman strength

Winter in the savanna seemed to be dragging for Kintaro and he longed for the summer when the rains would arrive and the replenishing of roots, grasses, and fruits, would make long nomadic treks more appealing.

However, he didn't complain and appreciated the healthy well-balanced ecosystem he lived in.

He was constantly worried about the survival of his kind from attacks by predators, and about humans' obsession with killing them for their tusks and confiscating land god had intended for animals.

Kintaro had been born albino, but had never been ridiculed by his peers for being different. Even though he was not yet an elder he was held in high esteem by the elders within the herd, mainly because of his wisdom and strength.

He was often called upon to deal with a ruckus or two between ambitious, delinquent bulls challenging for a more senior role within the herd.

They were a nomadic species, and the time had come for them to move on.

Kintaro felt that the herd had meandered too close to a Maasai village, where men, women, and children lived and worked the land for food. The herd being too close to them was dangerous.

Human casualties trodden to death by elephants were on the increase, so moving away would allow the humans to live without the threat of his herd nearby.

Today was a pivotal day, important from the elders' point of view. They were mostly females, given that the young bulls had left to find their own paths in life. It was an important day because Kintaro had asked to hold council and offer advice to the others as to their potential next steps.

Questions needed answering: how long they should stay where they were? Which direction they should take next? How could they escape men with guns and poisonous darts? How could they keep their distance from their neighbours, the Maasai villagers?

It was late afternoon and an ideal time for a meeting, as it was cooler.

The sun hung lower; there was relative silence and long shadows appeared beneath acacia trees.

The herd assembled, thirty elephants of all ages grunting and trumpeting in anticipation of words of wisdom, reassurance, and a sense of direction, to lead them towards the summer wet season, where the roots they foraged for on the flooded plains would be plentiful.

Silhouetted giraffes gracefully strolled by as if to eavesdrop on the meeting, or to gain some sort of survival intelligence.

Kandula, the matriarch, called for silence, as the elders Jaki, Elle, and Phyllis made their way to a kopje, which stood out like a small island in a sea of grasses.

Kintaro stepped forward from behind a group of seven- to eight-year-old bulls, who parted respectfully.

The last of the elders appeared, resembling royalty. They were the oldest members of the herd and often seen together; seldom were they apart.

Kanta and Luna were in their seventies. They had seen it all, some wonderful and some horrific days in the savannas, losing relatives alongside witnessing the arrivals of many new family members. In addition to their elder statesman roles, they helped to care for the young and served the herd well as emissaries with the odd rival herd.

Kandula stamped her authority once more and a hush descended upon the herd.

'Friends and family, thank you for your attendance. We live in a very different world from that of our ancestors and our numbers are in serious decline. It is important that we try to understand why this is happening and protect ourselves as much as we can. In the past, we worried about lack of food, the menace of the hyena, and the occasional hungry lion. Today, we face a very different threat in the form of poachers who crave our tusks for profit.

'There is also the prospect of our lands reducing at a rapid rate as landowners look to expand their territories, depriving us of much-needed water reserves.

'The outcome of this meeting and our next steps will be voted upon by the herd and a decision made by us all here today. I would like to invite Kintaro to speak about his thoughts and concerns on what we should do next.'

Kintaro entered the circle of elders and acknowledged every one of them.

He then turned to look at the others, outside the ring of elders, and addressed the whole group.

He cut straight to the chase. 'We are a nomadic species. For generations we have been constantly on the move to find new feeding grounds, safe havens to raise our children and teach our brightest to take on the mantle of the elders when they leave us.

'My recommendation is that we leave here within the next few days. The great migration of wildebeest is almost upon us and I feel that we should follow their lead, keeping a safe distance behind and emulating the success they have enjoyed for centuries. They will lead us to food and water. We can then evaluate the lands we encounter for safer, short-term settlements.'

Kintaro's words were absorbed by the herd, as though they were hearing god speak for the first time.

Respectful silence was followed by a trumpeting crescendo and the stamping of huge feet in appreciation of the words of wisdom they had just heard.

Once the applause had died down, Kandula thanked

Kintaro for his vision and, in true elephant tradition, asked him to temporarily leave the meeting, while his recommendations were considered and voted on by the others. He retired to the edge of the camp to gather his thoughts and plan the potential logistics involved for such a journey if positively voted for by the others.

As the sun went down and the late evening turned into a cool night, Kintaro welcomed the steady breeze, along with familiar sounds … a gentle low growl from a lion settling down for the night.

These were reassuring sounds that he was used to, but they were followed by an unnerving silence that he wasn't used to.

Something was wrong. It was too quiet.

He saw the glow of fires from the Maasai village, but all was quiet there.

There was a loud, piercing crack and a silvery flash of light from north of the large kopje, next to the herd.

The group was under attack.

It has to be poachers, he thought and immediately feared the impact this would have on a large group of elephants. A stampede was inevitable. Frightened elephants would flee in the opposite direction to where the shot had come from – in the direction of the Maasai village.

The villagers were in grave danger from a terrified group of elephants, a combined weight of thirty elephants fleeing for their lives and not caring about who or what lay in their way.

Kintaro had to do something; it would be a matter of minutes before the stampeding herd reached the village, where its inhabitants would not stand a chance. Having a head start, he raced towards the village, sounding the alarm as he went to awaken and warn the villagers.

He assumed a position at the entrance of the village, which consisted of numerous kraals, cattle pens, and crop patches. Kintaro's only hope was that his herd would recognise him and change direction. He prayed that they would not trample him and the villagers to death.

By now, the villagers had raised the alarm and panic ensued. Children awoke from their beds, terrified, clinging to their mothers. The men gathered what weapons they could, but realised it would be futile against a stampede of elephants.

However, the chief of the tribe spotted the huge thirteen-foot white elephant assuming a defensive position in front of the village entrance, ready to face the oncoming threat.

'Get behind the great white elephant!' the chief shouted, instinctively anticipating what Kintaro was trying to achieve. 'It's our only chance.'

The villagers responded by cowering behind the bulky, muscular frame of Kintaro. Within seconds, the stampede arrived – two, three, four adult elephants charging towards Kintaro.

'Stay behind me,' yelled Kintaro to the frightened villagers. He let out the loudest trumpeting alarm he could muster in an attempt to communicate with his out-of-control friends hurtling towards him.

But it was in vain; the charging elephants were too startled to hear and were almost upon him. Kintaro knew he would have to engage each one of his herd as they approached and use his size and strength to divert them away from the petrified villagers.

The first bull elephants were painfully deflected away by Kintaro and followed by others, narrowly missing him but obliterating huts and vegetable patches as they if they were never there.

The next wave of beasts appeared and Kintaro skilfully body checked them just as he had broken up young bull elephants' fights in the past. He heard desperate cries and screams from the frightened, defenceless villagers he was protecting.

Still they came, more and more charging elephants; the defence was now starting to take its toll on Kintaro, his body taking a battering. But still he held firm.

As the nightmare unfolded, a strange feeling came over Kintaro and he felt the need to look up to the night sky. There he saw the outline of a martial eagle, circling overhead and seemingly taking in the drama beneath him.

Narok was aware of what Kintaro was trying to do to save the villagers.

Kintaro's strength and resolve were diminishing. Some of the stampeding elephants were on a course to miss him, but would still destroy the homes of the villagers. There would be nothing left, only rubble, but so far no casualties thanks to his courage.

The eagle let out an audible cry like a clap of thunder. At that precise moment, Kintaro felt a weird sensation running through his entire body; he could only describe it as a shiver starting at his feet, quickly rising up to the top of his head.

Instinctively, he rose to his hind legs and stood upright, enhancing his huge muscular physique. No longer did he feel the pain of his engagements with the herd, nor did he feel fatigued at all – quite the opposite.

The next bull elephant raced towards Kintaro.

The villagers must have feared that they were doomed. Kintaro administered a blow with his new-found inner strength, which sent the raging elephant hurtling away from the villagers and rendering it unbalanced and facing the opposite direction.

This happened again and again, Kintaro now defending the villagers with ease until the stampede had ended and the villagers were safe. Calm was restored once again among the Maasai people and thanks heaped upon their hero, who had saved them from certain death.

Kintaro tried to make some sense of what had just happened. It had felt as if he had been given a gift – a new-found power to help do some good with his life – and the martial eagle had to have something to do with it.

Seconds later Narok appeared and hovered next to Kintaro's huge battle-weary head and spoke. 'You did well, Kintaro.'

'How do you know my name – and what happened to me back there?'

'My name is Narok and I have been sent by the gods of the savanna to give you a message.'

'What message?'

'The message is in the form of a quest, the nature of which will become apparent in the days to come. Your time with your herd has been completed and you have been an important influence in their survival. However, you must now leave them and follow a new path, a new adventure and ultimately your destiny. The gods have plans for you and three others.'

'What plans, what others? And what exactly did you do to me earlier?'

'I have already said that your destiny will be revealed soon. As for what happened earlier, the gods have bestowed upon you a gift of incredible strength, not only physical strength but also the mental fortitude to lead the others and ensure that you all complete your quest. I will leave you now, but say your goodbyes to your herd and trust in your instincts from here. I will never be far away and we will meet again soon.'

Narok ascended into the night sky leaving Kintaro trying to make sense of what had just happened.

He made his way back to the elders, joined along the way by some of his friends who moments before might unwittingly have caused him and the Maasai people harm. They did not appear to have completely understood what had unfolded, but bore no malice towards him at all. The scene was unusually sombre, and there was little communication between the elephants.

Kintaro reported on the events to the assembled elders, explained that he had personally experienced some kind of calling, triggered by the eagle, and that he must leave the herd immediately. He was not entirely sure why, but he had an overwhelming desire to find out what lay ahead for him.

3

Nakano

Japanese warrior

'Run, Nakano, run,' shouted Leena, Nakano's mother.

'I'm running, Mother, as fast as I can, but I can't keep up,' Nakano replied.

The herd was being chased by two helicopters with men hanging half in and half out of the fuselage. Nakano had already witnessed her cousin Grace being captured by men hurtling weighted nets over her and bringing her down to the ground beneath, her parents too frightened to stop and help.

'I'm tiring, Mother, I don't think I can run much further,' said Nakano.

'You must, Nakano, you must try.'

The helicopters swooped even lower, just missing the tops of trees, as the herd tried to escape to the relative protection offered by the bush.

The noise was deafening and incredibly frightening for a two-month-old calf, struggling to see where she was going with all the dust the helicopter's blades were whipping up. Nakano was exhausted and disorientated and had now strayed away from the herd and into a clearing, so the advantage of the chase shifted to her potential captors. Her strength and resilience had all but gone when she felt the weight of her assailants' net on top of her.

She tripped and rolled over several times. Nakano's heart felt as though it was going to burst out of her chest and she succumbed to the realisation that she had been caught. The prospect of not seeing her mother and family again completely overwhelmed her. She lay motionless on the ground, frozen with fear, and within minutes she heard the voices of her captors, shouting out orders to one another.

'Right, get the truck and the cage here,' one man shouted in a South African accent.

'Yes, Mr Duplessis, it's close, boss,' another answered.

Nakano was surrounded by men, mostly local men of colour she had seen before, but two white men seemed to be giving orders to the group.

It was all too much for the little elephant and she passed out.

***

The first thing Nakano saw when she awoke was the inside of a wooden cage. Through gaps between the slats she could see a road ahead and the plains to the sides. The cage contained straw and wood shavings, presumably for a bed, and some oranges next to a water trough that was only half full. The other half had sloshed out when the truck had driven over uneven road surfaces and was now evaporating in the blistering heat.

The journey seemed to last forever, but she estimated they had been travelling for two days by road when the vehicle eventually came to a stop.

Nakano tried to see where she was through the gaps in the cage, and she caught a glimpse of a mass of water, the size of which she had never seen before. Her only recollection of lots of water was bathing in a lake. This was different; the steady ripple of waves seemed to go on forever, with no trees or land on the horizon.

Where am I, where are we going? she thought. Not knowing her fate added to her anxiety. Suddenly, she felt herself being elevated and the cage rocked gently from side to side. The cage had been slowly hoisted into the air, and she saw structures and other vehicles the likes of which she had never seen before.

The cage swung out in a different direction towards the mass of water. As the cage rocked gently from side to side, she felt it lowering into what looked like a huge dark hole, coming to rest near to other cages and crates, which contained lions, cheetahs, giraffes and zebra, all cramped in separate crates, but closer than they would have liked to be in their natural habitat.

It was an unnerving, surreal experience for an elephant of her tender years, and one Nakano could not understand. The next thing she heard was voices again, the same voices she'd heard shouting at one another when she was first kidnapped.

'Make sure it is fed and watered – the zoo will not pay top rand for a skinny elephant.'

'Okay, boss, no problem, Mr Duplessis,' said one of the captors.

'I'm frightened,' came a very faint call from the crate closest to her. 'What will happen to us?' The voice came from a lion cub, cowering in the corner of an oversized crate.

'I don't know and I'm scared too,' said Nakano, 'but let's try and be brave.'

'I miss my mother and I'm hungry. She normally feeds me by now,' said the lion cub.

'What's your name, little lion?' Nakano asked.

'My name is Boots. What is your name?'

'Why did your mother call you Boots?' said Nakano.

'My mother said that I have feet the size of gumboots,' he replied.

'I see … my name is Nakano.'

'What does that mean?' Boots asked.

'My mother once told me that my name was taken from a famous Japanese warrior who fought in the Boshin War and led a band of female fighters. She was reported to have defeated hundreds of samurai warriors.'

'Wow,' said Boots, 'and do you want to grow up like her?'

'I would like to be brave, so you and I need to follow her example and get through this,' Nakano replied.

'I hope we stay together, Naki. Is it okay if I call you Naki?' asked Boots.

'Of course you can call me Naki, but only you,' said Nakano.

This made Boots feel very privileged and relieved that he had met someone he felt would look after him.

Nakano and her new friend came to the conclusion that they were away from dry land and had no idea where they were being taken. They assumed that the mass of water could be a huge lake and that they were destined for somewhere far from their families and homes.

****

Nakano and her fellow fugitives had no idea how long they had been travelling.

Many of the animals were sick and weary from the journey, but they had been well fed, watered, and not mistreated in any way. The journey seemed like a lifetime to them, which caused further stress when they arrived at their destination and were herded onto lorries for yet another trek by land.

Where are we going now? Nakano thought.

Fortunately, it was just a short journey and only took a couple of hours.

Safari World on the outskirts of Bangkok was the new home for Boots and Nakano. It did not take them long to realise that their new habitat in no way resembled the peace and tranquillity of the savanna plains.

The two friends could see all kinds of animals they

were familiar with and some they had never seen before, but what was most disconcerting for them was seeing how these animals were restricted as to where they could roam. Nakano saw white tigers pacing up and down behind most peculiar metal fences. Inside those fences the land lacked vegetation with barren areas and no trees, shrubs or long grasses she was accustomed to living and feeding among.

***

Boots and Nakano met some dear friends, though, during their ten-year stay at Safari World, most notable being Monty the Orangutan.

Monty or Master Monty, M&M as his friends often called him, was especially protective of Boots and Nakano.

He demanded respect from all, who referred to him as the master, due to the amazing array of self-defence skills he had acquired before his capture in Borneo fifteen years ago.

Monty had perfected the arts of tai chi, muay tai, capoeira, Shaolin kung fu, and laido, which he was more than willing to teach his two new-found friends, to help protect them and keep under his wing.

Nakano developed an incredible aptitude for laido, the most deadly martial art involving a weapon, but despite her size, she had become very adept, too, at capoeira, teaching the body to use its limbs and the ground to inflict kicks with devastating effect.

As time went by, Nakano felt that life at Safari World had become even more desperate, food started to run short and the numbers of humans visiting had diminished. Perhaps this was the reason why the people responsible for looking after them could no longer afford to feed them, and sadly several species of inmates perished through hunger, dehydration, or lack of medication needed to ward off infection.

She knew something was seriously wrong and her fears were confirmed one day when a number of lorries, trucks and cars, all of the same colour, entered the park, stopping at the building where the staff at the park usually gathered. Men and women wearing white coats got out of their vehicles and congregated outside the building and seemed to be listening to information relayed by one individual who looked to be in charge of whatever was happening.

The individual was a mature gentleman with white hair and a beard and the only human not dressed in a white coat.

After a short period of time the group of white-coated humans split up and made their way to several of the animal enclosures, some getting back into trucks and venturing further into the park.

It became apparent to Nakano that the previous owners were no longer in charge and that her future and that all of the other animals was uncertain.

To her surprise, the gentleman with the white hair made his way to the compound where she was tethered in chains to a concrete post. He approached the fence and spoke to her. 'Please don't be afraid,' he said, 'My name is Dr Max and I mean you no harm. I want you to know that I am here today with help, to take you home where you belong.'

Nakano stared at him, not knowing whether to trust him. Was he another greedy zoo owner, ready to unveil his latest attraction somewhere equally as terrible? Or could she trust him? 'How do I know that you are telling the truth? I don't know you. I have never seen you before. How can I trust any human again?' she asked.

'Not all humans are bad people. I care deeply about elephants and have devoted most of my life to the conservation and survival of endangered species. I am proud to be the founder of an organisation dedicated to finding areas within Africa where you and your relatives can be safe and protected,' said Dr Max.

'My name is Nakano – is it only elephants you care about?' she asked.

'My particular passion is for elephants, yes, but I am part of a group of wonderful people who are also committed to the survival of endangered species around the world. Collectively, we are working with the people who run countries to not only ensure the survival of our precious animal kingdom but of our planet too.'

Nakano was struggling to understand everything the man was saying and she had many questions she wanted to ask him, which came out quite randomly.

'How will you get me home?' she said.

'We have specialist transport already here, with animal doctors to accompany you on your journey back to Africa,' the doctor replied.

'I'm not leaving without Boots,' said Nakano.

'You wear boots? That is most unusual,' said Dr Max.

'No, Boots is my friend.'

'I was not aware there was another elephant in the park.'

'Boots is not an elephant, he is a lion, and where I go, he goes!'

'Okay, Naki,' said the doctor.

'Don't call me Naki!'

'My apologies, Nakano, I did not mean to offend you. Of course, Boots can come with you, but will it not be too dangerous, a lion and an elephant on board ship together?' said Dr Max.

'Boots is just fine with me and will behave himself. Trust me this time.'

'Okay, I will make the arrangements,' said the doctor.

'Just one other thing,' said Nakano. 'Boots and I have one other friend in the park called Monty, Master Monty. He is an amazing orangutan and needs to go home to Borneo.'

'We have seen to that. Among us today is a wonderful lady called Mrs Kenna, who has already secured a place for your friend at the Semenggoh Wildlife Rehabilitation Centre in Borneo. He will be safe there and back to his home,' Dr Max replied.

The three friends were allowed to meet up and

Nakano and Boots said goodbye to Monty, wished him well, and hoped that one day they might see each other again.

***

Nakano and Boots knew what to expect on the long journey home, even though the first journey had been ten years ago.

Their cage was much larger and more comfortable this time, made out of steel, with plenty of room, water, straw, and food. Boots was fed regularly with fresh meat, after which he slept most of the time, snoring to his heart's content.

The cage, however, had to be locked for the crew's safety. Boots was now a fully grown and extremely dangerous lion.

On the voyage, Nakano had plenty of time to think about what the future held for her and Boots. She also realised that they would be parted once they reached Africa. Boots needed to live a very different life from that of the elephant community and she hoped he would never chance his arm at one of her kind for dinner!

As for Dr Max, he vowed to meet them in a month, once the ship docked, to ensure they connected with the next leg of their journey home.

About twenty days into the voyage, Boots was sleeping as usual when Nakano heard some unusual voices, foreign voices she had not heard before, followed by rapid gunfire and explosions.

What's happening, surely we can't be under attack again? she thought. Nakano had heard gunshots before, with the so-called 'putting to sleep' of fellow inmates at Safari World.

There was a lot of commotion, people shouting, screaming and more gunfire. What was happening? She was getting worried.

Boots was awakened by the noise. 'What's going on, Naki?' he asked.

'I'm not sure, Boots, but I don't like it,' she said.

The hold door opened and Pierre the vet fell through it, clutching a gunshot wound in his side. Behind him, the pair could see the stairs filled with fire and the faint glimmer of daylight sky up above.

Nakano caught glimpses of several people of very dark skin running above deck and carrying weapons. These were people she had not seen when they first boarded ship and could only assume they were trying to kidnap the animals and take control of the ship by force.

'Please make this be a bad dream,' said Boots. 'I cannot take more bad luck and uncertainty.'

'Try and stay calm, Boots. It's not a dream and we will get through this,' said Nakano, trying to reassure him.

She kept her eyes peeled on the stairs from the hold, trying to decide what to do next. Apart from the obvious panic among the crew with people running, sometimes falling, she caught a glimpse of a large bird circling above.

Nakano had seen many birds in her time and this particular bird was familiar, but not in its usual place. It was an eagle, out at sea. 'How could that happen?' she thought. But the eagle vanished as quickly as it had appeared.

'We need to do something, Boots, the fire from the stairs is getting stronger and spreading into our space,' she said.

'But we're locked in, Naki, we'll burn to death,' said Boots.

'Keep calm, we have to stay calm and think.'

'Naki, I don't wish to further alarm you, but see that crate over there by the foot of the stairs, it's got explosives written on the side and the flames are getting closer to it.'

'We need to get out,' said Nakano, stating the obvious.

'But how, Naki?'

'We have to somehow get that crate out first.'

'How? We're locked in a cage and the crate's already caught fire. We're going to die.'

'Try cheering me up, why don't you,' said Nakano sarcastically.

No sooner had he stopped jabbering than Nakano saw the eagle circling in the sky above the stairs for a second time. This time she remembered what it was – she had seen them before in the savanna. It was a martial eagle, suspended in the sky, and it was looking at her.

Seconds later, Nakano felt what she could only describe as an out-of-body experience, which passed in a flash. Something had come over her and she felt numb, cold, causing her to shiver, but strangely enlightened.

'What just happened to me?' she said.

'What are you talking about Naki? We're about to be blown to bits,' said Boots.

In what appeared to be a bizarre pause in time, Nakano wished she could somehow move the crate to the starboard side of the hold, away from their cage. To her amazement, the crate of dynamite levitated on its own and shot across the hold like a burning fireball, smashing against the starboard wall.

In a split second it exploded, blowing a huge hole in the ship's side. The two friends thought they were dead, blown to pieces from the blast, but incredibly, they survived. The smoke and devastation all around were enormous, but they were alive.

'How did that happen, Naki? The crate moved on its own – did you do it?' Boots asked.

'I don't know – I just wished it would happen to give us a fighting chance,' she said.

'Well, thank the gods it did. But we now have another problem.'

'What's that?' she replied.

'Water … the hold's filling up with water and we're still locked in this cage. We've survived being blown up, but now we'll probably drown.'

'You are an optimist, Boots. There has to be a key. Quick, look around, see if you can see where it's kept,' said Nakano.

'I can't see anything other than smoke and I'm now finding it difficult to breathe.'

'Keep looking, our lives depend on it, Boots. Lions are supposed to have incredible senses, aren't they?' Nakano said.

'Wait.' Through a gap in the smoke, Boots could see a set of keys attached to a circular ring the circumference of a grapefruit hanging from a hook.

'There, Naki, hanging from that desk. Can you see them?'

'I can, Boots. Well done.'

'But how will we retrieve them?' he asked. 'Perhaps we need a stick or something to unhook it.'

'Can you see a stick, Boots? Because I can't?'

'Make them come to us as you did with the crate,' said Boots.

'I'm not even sure I did that ... perhaps it was an initial detonation that sent it hurtling across the room?'

'No, it was you, I'm sure of it. Try, Naki, try.'

Nakano was out of answers, so she thought again about her experience with the eagle and tried to will the keys towards them. Initially there was nothing, no movement whatsoever.

'Concentrate, Naki, you can do it – concentrate,' said Boots.

Nakano knew it was their only hope and cleared her mind of everything other than somehow making the keys come to them. If she had influenced the crate moving, perhaps she could do it again, this time with the keys.

The water levels were now getting dangerously high and it would not be long before the hold was submerged.

She started to concentrate and focus.

Sure enough, the keys moved. They levitated and unhooked themselves to be held suspended miraculously in mid-air.

'See, Naki, I knew you could do it.'

Nakano intensified her focus even more and, to her amazement, the keys floated across the hold unaided towards the cage, to the point where Nakano grabbed them with her outstretched trunk.

'You've got them, Naki, you did it,' said Boots.

Nakano decided to try each of the keys on the loop. Fortunately, the first key she tried opened the cage door and the two friends were free. Their only escape now was through the hole the explosives had created and take their chances in the sea.

'Let's jump, on the count of three,' said Nakano. 'One, two, three.'

The two friends landed in the sea, Nakano making the biggest splash for obvious reasons. Boots, however, hated the prospect of being submerged and coughed and spluttered as he came to the surface.

When he gained his composure and started to swim, it wasn't long before he found a sizeable piece of debris to cling to, but Nakano was nowhere to be seen.

What chance would a three-ton elephant have in choppy waters, he thought and started to panic, calling for his friend. 'Naki, Naki!'

'What's all this yelling about?' said Nakano from behind him.

'Thank the gods you're alive, Naki, I thought you had drowned.'

'Don't you know that elephants make excellent swimmers, Boots?' she said.

'No, I did not,' he replied. 'You're too fat to float.'

'Cheeky.'

'So what do we do now?' said Boots.

'We float and wait, and hopefully, someone will pick us up soon.'

***

As if their adventure could not get any more surreal, they were soon joined by the martial eagle Nakano saw from the ship.

It settled down on the debris next to Boots, facing the swimming Nakano. To their surprise, it started to speak.

'Nakano, I have to tell you that the strange events you and your friend have just experienced happened for a reason. You will no doubt be wondering how you were able to save yourselves from certain death and feeling confused as to what you made happen. My name is Narok and you are the third in a group of four Heavenly Kings who have been chosen. I have granted each one of you a special power. This will help you and the group to fulfil a destiny. You will meet the others when the time is right and complete the quartet to be known as the Tamonten Tusks. My work is done here, but fear not, your spell of good fortune will continue.'

Narok flew away and into the distance.

Sure enough, their good fortune did continue; a couple of hours later, they were picked up by a Greenpeace vessel, which was alerted about the pirates in the area and the attack on a ship.

Nakano and Boots reached the port of Maputo a few days later, where Dr Max was waiting for them with transport to individually take them home.

Boots hugged Nakano tearfully and they said their goodbyes, having shared an incredible friendship and adventure. They agreed that their paths would hopefully cross again; it would be sad to think otherwise.

4

Yuki-Onna

Yuki

Yuki-Onna liked her name, especially the shortened version, Yuki.

Her parents had once explained that it was her mother's fascination with Japanese culture and especially Japanese folklore that influenced her choice of names.

Yuki-Onna was known as the Snow Woman by the Renga poet named Sogi. Legend had it that once a beautiful woman came to visit a man and became his wife, because the woman desired it. This woman was reluctant to go into a bath. When she was made to go in anyway, she disappeared, leaving only thin fragmented floating icicles.

This was Yuki's favourite story because it made her feel mysterious. What had happened to the Snow Woman, where did she go and would she reappear?

In her early years of learning Yuki's parents, especially her mother, taught her many things, not only compassion for others, but culture, the importance of the environment, the survival of her species and those of her contemporaries in the savannas being of utmost relevance.

Her fondest memories, however, were of her mother reading to her before bedtime. Most of Yuki's herd did not entirely get what she was 'into'. They respected her intelligence though and she was often seen alone, writing poetry. Yuki was occasionally called upon to compose romantic messages for the young bull elephants to send to sweethearts from other herds, via the bush telegraph. Her reward was plentiful supplies of food but without the foraging.

However, her concern of late was not just the impact of the ivory trade, but the threat of legalised hunting. Wealthy game hunters from the United States, in particular, were hunting exceptional specimens of lions, elephants, cheetahs, and rhino, targeting the finest examples and negatively influencing animal genes vital to the sustainability of their species.

She understood that campaigners for legalised hunting would argue that substantial monies went to local communities, but questioned whether that happened within corrupt governments. Nor could she ever concede that legalised hunting would help conserve the future of her species. She would never condone the activity as a sport, nor did she see it as something the gods would have wanted either.

Yuki felt she had a duty to help protect endangered species and use her intellect to try and educate humans against the enterprise and help to find a solution.

After all, the fact remained that the ecosystem they lived amongst had survived for generations, and it was the humans' greed and self-indulgence that had tipped the balance.

Yuki's herd were relatively safe for now within the confines of the Tarangire National Park, where they felt protected. However, being nomadic, they were prone to wandering and could stray too close to the border of the park.

The boundary to the south was not protected and considered 'fair game' by the hunters, leaving the herd vulnerable. This critical quandary was a topic of discussion for the elders of the herd, where Yuki was occasionally a valued participant, even though she was not an elder, but more of an advisor.

Today was another discussion day and Yuki was invited to attend. Fulande, the most respected of the elders, highlighted the topic to the group. *'Staying safe.* Yuki, this is your opportunity to address the group with your views relating to our ultimate safety and security.'

Yuki stepped forward nervously; she was not yet used to addressing such esteemed individuals. She realised that what she was about to say could offend some of the wise old owls in the group.

'My need to speak out about this subject is sincere. We know about the threat of predator animals within the savanna and we have experienced the covert tactics of the poacher, for which we keep a watchful eye. But I feel it my duty to make you aware of an equally worrying threat, which is that of the hunter – in the name of so-called sport. These people are not interested in our tusks, nor are they concerned with our skins for medicines. Their motivation is to take a part of us home, as a trophy,' she said.

The assembled group simultaneously let out a distressed trumpeting call and stamped their feet in exasperation.

'How many more threats to our lives here must we endure?' said Winston, Fulande's chief advisor.

'I agree, we should not let them change our way of life. Those paths and instincts have seen us survive many generational difficulties – drought, disease, famine …' said Safi, who had seen it all.

'Please listen to me,' said Yuki. 'The fact remains that we are currently too close to the park border. We need to move north and quickly.'

'Why should we flee now? What's the rush? We know which path to take,' said Winston.

'That path could be one of danger, of loss of life. My only suggestion is that we head north, well into the relative safety of the Tarangire, with only the poachers to worry about,' said Yuki.

'We could take our chances south of the border,' said Winston.

'The people who help these hunters need the money and are cunning. They will set bait for lions to cross the line. They will bang drums and create noise to frighten and steer us into the direction of their high-powered rifles,' Yuki advised.

Fulande interrupted with authority and she demanded order from the group. 'Yuki has alerted us to a very serious threat, one we have not encountered before, for which we are indebted to her. Yuki, thank you for your caution.'

Yuki bowed her head respectfully and retired to the periphery of the camp. Whilst collecting her thoughts, a strange thing happened to her, which neither frightened nor shocked her. A martial eagle circled above, then swooped down and came to land right beside her.

It began to speak. 'Hello, Yuki, my name is Narok – please don't be alarmed.'

'What do you want and how do you know my name?' she asked. 'I've never met an eagle before.'

'I have been watching you for some time, Yuki, and you interest me enormously,' said Narok.

'What do you mean?' said Yuki.

'You will not know this yet, but you have been chosen by the gods. There is a purpose to your life that is already mapped out for you. I am here to ensure that you achieve it.'

'What purpose?' Yuki asked.

'You have been chosen to join three others and complete a quest to ensure the survival of our biome and to find a solution to man's obsession with killing endangered animals,' said Narok.

'But how can I help? I am but a mere cow elephant. Educated, maybe, but poachers and hunters are too much of a match for me.'

'Your role is very important and I see you as the voice of the foursome.'

'I am but a hefty African cow elephant! Not exactly the kind of delegate who would sit at the table of an important government meeting,' said Yuki.

'Agreed, but I have already bestowed upon you a gift – a gift that you already feel familiar with.'

'What gift,' Yuki asked impatiently.

'You remember the Snow Woman?' said Narok.

'Yes, of course I do.'

'What happened to her?' Narok asked.

'She disappeared in a bath, leaving slivers of icicles,' Yuki replied.

'Well, the gods have given me the power to grant you the ability to disappear at will,' said Narok.

'Like Yuki-Onna in Japanese folklore?'

'Yes. This power will enable you to covertly attend poacher and hunter briefings, but more importantly official meetings, without being seen, but certainly being heard,' said Narok.

'How will I know when this will happen to me?' said Yuki.

'You will need to summon it from within. But take note, it will be short-lived. When in an invisible state you will need to act quickly, get your point across or listen for information, then leave promptly.'

'You mentioned three others. Who are they and when will I meet them?'

'All in good time. You are the last of the four I have

entrusted with special powers and your paths will cross very soon. That's all I can tell you for now and your appreciation of their given talents will become apparent.'

Narok wished Yuki well, reassured her that he would never be far away, and soared off into the sky. She tried to make sense of the conversation she had just had with Narok and understand how it left her feeling. Confusion, for sure; was this happening to her? Or could it be a dream and she had fallen asleep for a short time? If it was true, how would she call upon this gift and when or how would she eventually meet the others?

Yuki decided that she needed some additional time, a change of environment. She often went for a walk when she needed to get things straight in her head, so she headed off aimlessly to get some solitude and collect her thoughts.

After daydreaming for some time, she found herself in an area of the bush she did not recognise and in a densely populated area of long grasses, acacia trees, and a collection of kopjes shimmering in the early evening sun of the savanna.

Yuki had drifted out of the relatively safe area of the Tarangire National Park and into the hazardous area, where the threat from game hunters was a reality. Instead of the normal evening bush bedlam and babbling, the mood seemed different, disquieting, and she began to feel a little threatened.

These were emotions Yuki was right to feel as she surveyed her whereabouts. Slowly turning in 360 degrees, she caught a glimpse of red light emanating from a shrub, then another caught her eye from the opposite direction. Yuki now felt fear; this was alien to the sights she was familiar with in the bush.

She heard the faintest of human voices, as if to signal others, a rustling of foliage, then simultaneously they appeared.

'Let's make this a three-party kill, guys.'

The three hunters raised their high-powered rifles, aiming them in Yuki's direction. She froze, unable to move and nowhere to run, even if she had been able to move. 'Think, Yuki, do something,' she said. *Wish I was … invisible right now*, she thought.

The sound of gunshots screeched, extinguishing the quiet that had gone before them, bullets travelling twice as fast as a cheetah at full speed.

Yuki had vanished!

'Where did it go?' said one of the men.

'What the hell just happened?' said another.

'It just vanished,' said the third.

Yuki had escaped just in time and now realised that the amazing gift Narok had given her had saved her life.

***

The three bewildered hunters returned to their camp empty-handed.

African guide Kwame made a fire and they settled down for some food and beer and to contemplate the bizarre event they had experienced just a short time before.

'I have never seen or experienced anything like that in my entire life,' said one of the hunters.

'Me neither,' said another, 'but there must be a logical explanation for it.'

'Crazy beast just vanished, that's all there is to it. It must be faster than we thought. Kwame, you promised us a damn elephant, man, and you failed to deliver.'

'Do not worry, boss, I have a plan for tomorrow. With some help from my friends in the village, we will create a diversion with drums and cymbals, then lure the herd I was telling you about away from the Tarangire and beyond the reserve. You will have the pick of the herd and as many trophies as you like,' said Kwame.

'You better be right, or you're not getting a single rand out of us,' one of the men threatened.

Yuki, in her invisible form, had positioned herself near to the group and heard every word of the plan for the next day. How could she stop this from happening and would she get back to the herd in time, to warn them? She needed to ensure they stayed in the relative safety of the Tarangire.

I have to do something to slow the hunters down, or disarm them in some way, she thought.

Then she spied her opportunity.

To the rear of the camp and in front of the hunters' four-by-four pickup were their rifles, neatly arranged in a pyramid formation, with barrels pointing to the night sky.

She then carefully entered the camp, gingerly making her way towards the weapons and trying not to make a noise, which was not an easy task. When she reached the stockpile, she leapt into the air and landed with her huge feet on top of the rifles, smashing them to pieces as if they were a bunch of twigs readied to make a fire.

The four men rose to their feet and ran towards the commotion to discover that their rifles were destroyed, with no explanation as to how it had happened.

'I'm getting out of here tomorrow, guys. This godforsaken country is freaking me out,' said of the men.

Yuki's work was done and her instincts helped her make her way back to the herd, gradually becoming more visible as she walked.

Shortly after returning, she was asked to join the group again, to hear the outcome of the discussion.

'We have listened to your argument, Yuki and have decided to take heed of your warning and set a course north, further into the Tarangire,' said Fulande.

'I'm so glad. You will be safer there, but I have to inform you of a decision I have made too, about myself,' she replied.

'And what is that?' asked Fulande.

'I have decided to leave the herd and follow an undertaking bestowed upon me to join others in a quest from the gods.'

'Well, how are you going to do that, Yuki?' said Winston disrespectfully.

Yuki instantly vanished. 'That's how,' she said, to the complete astonishment of the others.

5

Professor Gon and Clem

Brains meet brawn

Professor Gon was not surprised that cutbacks had meant the university could only afford to send him on his latest research visit by way of a tourist safari package. Consequently, he thought he would be among so-called wild animal lovers whose main interest would probably be where the hotel bar and swimming pool were located and in that order.

Gon was a stereotypical English gentleman – a monocle-wearing, stiff-upper-lipped, intelligent fox with an ironic sense of humour. This often got him into trouble with people less well versed in matters relating to the environment, politics, and religion. A Molotov cocktail if ever there was one.

His main objective for the visit was to spend time studying not only elephants but other endangered species, such as the black rhino. As far back as 1970, the black rhino numbered 65,000 in Africa, but twenty or so years later had diminished to only 2,300, due mainly to poaching. Gon's schedule was planned in advance. He intended to catch up with other zoologists, conservationists, national park rangers and members of local communities.

On the first day of the safari the professor had risen, as he always did, at five. He spent time ensuring he looked immaculate, donning very sensible attire consisting of a khaki insect-proof jacket and long trousers, hiking boots, the compulsory Akubra Coober Pedy hat, and a beige leather rucksack containing everything from bug spray to heartburn tablets. The final and most important accessory was his Zeiss binoculars, which were as good today as they had been twenty years ago.

'I say, old chap, you most certainly look the part,' he said, admiring himself in the full-length mirror in his room.

Gon was not in the least bit surprised to be the first to arrive at the open-topped four-by-four Land Rovers parked outside the hotel reception and ready to leave at 5.30 a.m. sharp. The bush looked serene; it was still quite dark and a little misty, but enchanting all the same.

Four men dressed in uniform, whom he assumed to be the guides and drivers, were standing smoking in front of the vehicles.

'A very good morning to you, fine gentleman,' Gon said to the men, who seemed surprised to have been acknowledged, but responded courteously.

The professor took his seat in one of the vehicles and pondered who would accompany him on the day's tour. *I do hope everyone will turn up on time*, he thought.

First to arrive, and on time, were what looked like a husband and wife couple, probably from Australia, he thought. Not because he was some sort of people-watching psychologist, but because they were both dressed the same and wearing matching cork hats, with the gentleman brandishing a can of Tooheys lager in his hand.

'G' day cobber, how ya doin', mate? Me name's Shane and this is me Sheila, Sheila,' said the Aussie chap.

'Very pleased to meet you, Shane, but what is your wife … or Sheila's name?' Gon said politely.

'It's Sheila like I said, mate, are you deaf?' said Shane.

'No, absolutely not,' Gon replied. 'I thought Sheila was an affectionate pseudonym for a wife or partner in Australia.'

'What's a sumo's name got to do with anything?' asked Shane.

'Don't worry, Shane, I think I get it. Nice to make your acquaintance, Shelia. My name is Gon.'

'Gone where?' Sheila joked, and laughed with what resembled a hyena's cackle.

'No, not gone anywhere, my dear, my name is Gon, Professor Gon, to be precise.'

'I knew that, mate,' Sheila replied, 'only kidding.'

Shane turned to his wife and said, 'Sure looking forward to seeing some boomers in the bush today, Shee.'

'Me too, Shanie,' Sheila replied.

'And pray what are boomers?' Gon asked.

'Oh, it's your first time, hey cobber? Bless him, Shee,

he doesn't even know a large roo when he sees one,' said Shane.

'If you are referring to the marsupial known as the kangaroo from the Macropodidae family, my dear fellow, you will not see one in this bush,' said Gon.

'Crikey, Shee, we've paid bucketloads of dollars and they haven't even got any roos here,' said Shane.

At that point, they were joined by two other members of the group, who boarded the four-by-four in a very considered and elegant fashion.

'*Buon giorno, tutti*,' said the handsome debonair-looking man.

'What's he say, Shee?' Shane asked of his wife.

'I've not a scooby doo what the hell they're talking about, Shanie,' said Sheila.

'*Buon giorno, signore e signora*,' Gon replied.

'May I introduce to you my bella Sofia,' the man said proudly.

'And this is *mi amore*, Fabio,' said Sofia.

'Strewth, Shee, think they must be Spanish or Russian,' Shane said quietly in his wife's ear.

The graceful Italian couple took their seats and Gon checked his pocket watch. It was now 5.20 a.m. and there were still two empty seats, excluding one for the driver and one for the guide at the front. The other four-by-four was full and waiting for Gon's Land Rover to complete its manifest before the party could head off.

The professor's party chatted among themselves in anticipation of an eventful day as the minutes passed by and beyond five thirty. Gon was becoming quite agitated; he was a stickler for punctuality and questioned the driver, who by now had finished all his cigarettes and taken his seat.

'Excuse me, young man. Have you any idea where the remaining passengers are?' he said. The driver's head disappeared into his shoulders in response.

It was now approaching 6 a.m. and, at last, emerging from one of the lodges, were what looked like two newlyweds, clinging on to each other like conjoined twins. Both were inappropriately dressed, wearing flip-flops, shorts, and skin-tight T-shirts. Designer sunglasses were strategically placed above the bride's forehead and she was clasping the very latest smartphone in one hand and a very hygienic-looking water receptacle in the other.

Not equipped at all for the day ahead, Gon thought, but could not help himself from questioning their tardiness. 'Excuse me for interrupting your morning stroll,' he said sarcastically. 'But did you not get the instruction to be here at five thirty, like everyone else?'

'Sorry, mate,' the boy answered. 'It's our honeymoon and Robyn likes a little nap after breakfast. It's our first holiday away from England together.'

'I see – and any thoughts about the rest of us waiting patiently here for you to arrive?' said Gon.

'We did set the alarm for four thirty, but it takes me half an hour to straighten my hair,' the newlywed wife replied.

'Then she has to have at least three cups of coffee

before she can even speak,' said her husband.

'Oh, for god's sake, driver, let's get on or it will be sunset soon,' said Gon.

The two Land Rovers headed off into the bush in convoy, albeit half an hour late.

***

They had been driving for at least an hour when the dark and misty conditions quickly turned into warm sunshine with not a cloud in the sky. The Land Rover containing Gon's group was in the lead and it wasn't long before the tour guide gave up his seat next to the driver and, with a rifle in hand, moved onto the bonnet of the vehicle to get a better view.

The first glimpse of wildlife they encountered could not have been more exciting. They very slowly taxied towards a kopje with a lioness, her cubs resting by her side.

She must have fed them recently, Gon thought, because the lions showed no interest in their visitors at all.

However, everyone in the group reached for their digital cameras and mobile phones and started snapping away, paparazzi-style, and the constant clicking of shutters startled the cubs.

The two vehicles kept their distance and once the photoshoot was over, they drove off further into the bush.

Another two hours passed and, after the euphoria of the lion sighting, the bush wildlife seemed to have dried up. The group was now becoming impatient; they wanted to see elephants, zebra, impala, cheetahs, and hyenas, but all they could see were long grasses, acacia trees, and dust from the vehicles' tyres.

Just as the moans and groans were escalating, the mood changed in an instant, when the vehicle seemed to have been hit by what felt like a ten-ton truck.

'What the heck was that?' said Shane as the rest of the group screamed with fright.

The four-by-four started to topple over and its occupants were thrown to the ground beneath it. Panic set in as the startled tourists realised they had been charged by a rhino.

'Run for your lives,' said Fabio, helping his wife to her feet.

The two African guides had already fled, giving no thought for the paying guests they were charged to keep safe. The professor had also been unceremoniously thrown to the ground and was very dazed and bemused as to what had just happened. All he could see was his fellow passengers fleeing, with their arms in the air, towards the second four-by-four, which was still upright and positioned about a hundred metres away.

Gon was in shock and all alone. He picked himself up next to the four-by-four, which was on its side, and heard the haunting snort of a rhinoceros waiting to move in for the kill.

The rhino positioned itself for the second wave of the attack, which was aimed at the retreating tourists.

In a moment of complete madness, the professor moved away from the side of the vehicle so that the rhino could see him, and positioned himself between the rhino and the fleeing passengers.

It looked like a stand-off.

Gon and rhino, facing each other like a gunfight at the OK Corral.

'Move out of the way, fox,' said the rhino.

'I happen to have a name,' Gon replied.

'I don't give a buffalo's butt what your name is, fox. You look like a scrawny fox to me.'

'Let me introduce myself. My name is Gon, Professor Gon, to be precise.'

'As I said, I don't give a baboon's bottom what your name is. Move out of the way or I will mow you down too,' said the rhino.

'Now listen here, my good man,' said Gon. 'I'm getting quite annoyed now. Whatever do you think you can achieve by charging at us like a scene from *Bedknobs and Broomsticks*?'

'What's knob heads and toothpicks, fox? I've never heard of that,' the rhino replied.

'It's not important, my dear fellow. What is your name anyway? I can't keep calling you rhino.'

'Why should I tell you my name, squirt?'

'Because it's polite, fatty, that's why.' Gon was disappointed with himself having been reduced to the rhino's level of conversation.

'Don't you call me fatty, shrimp!'

'Well tell me your damn name, goof, and I will stop insulting you.'

'Okay, there's no harm in telling you my name before I demolish the lot of you. It's Clem.'

'That's better ... Clem. Now, answer one question for me. What is there to be gained by killing innocent people?'

'These people, as you call them, wiped out most of my friends and family,' said Clem.

'So, what do you think will happen if you kill people now? They will brand you a killer and hunt you down. Then there will be one less black rhino to count,' said Gon.

'Why should you care, Professor, and why are you protecting them?'

'I'm not protecting them. Can't you see? I'm trying to protect you! My whole purpose in life is to see endangered species such as yours flourish and to try and educate my fellow humans to find a way of ensuring that no more precious animals become extinct. I am a zoologist from England and I have studied wildlife for a very long time. It's the reason I travelled hundreds of miles to conduct my research and meet with people who can influence what goes on around here.'

'Is Elephand as far as the Kruger from here?' Clem asked.

'Much further away, and it is England, my dear fellow.'

By now the other tourists had fled the scene and been picked up by the second Land Rover.

'So, what happens now? I suppose you will need to

get back to your research,' said Clem.

'I will, Clem, but what about you? What will you do?' Gon asked.

'Oh, I guess I will try and continue with my life, find a wife, be on the run from poachers, hunters, continually looking over my shoulder and trying to grow eyes at the back of my head, what do you think, Prof?' said Clem sarcastically.

'And I thought I was sarcastic. Why don't you join me and we can fight for survival together? I'll be the brains, you be the brawn, and maybe we could make a difference, helping your neighbours out here? I can't believe that we are the only ones fighting this cause, and something tells me that fate will draw us to like-minded individuals who will also be championing the cause for endangered species.'

'Okay, Prof, what have I got to lose? I suppose you will need that truck to get you around and keep up with me? Let me get it upright for you. You can drive, can't you, Prof?'

Clem nudged the Land Rover upright and Gon climbed aboard to see if it would start. Fortunately, it started the first time and seemed not to have suffered much damage. *British engineering at his finest,* Gon thought.

The two new friends headed off into the late afternoon sun, Gon excited at the prospect of working with Clem's brawn coupled with his brains.

6

How Kintaro met Bosh

Defeating an ogre

Kintaro had been wandering for a considerable time since leaving his herd, but still felt as though he was being guided with each step he took.

The one thing he was sure about was a desperate need for water, not only to rehydrate but to wallow in a combination of mud and water to protect his skin from the blistering heat.

He chuckled to himself about the names he had thought of for a new sun protection lotion especially for elephants, like 'Mara Mud' or 'Swampy Skin'.

Just another nomadic trek, he thought, taking in the usual sights and sounds the plains had to offer. Life in the savanna, though, was never dull and from his height he was able to see other animals going about their business, usually feeding or chilling out.

Occasionally, he would witness the drama nature presented the catch-me-if-you-can hunt for food. Such a scenario was about to unfold and the peace and tranquillity of the plains would inevitably be disturbed. In the distance, he saw a cloud of dust emerging and getting closer to his location, along with the continuous thud of hooves, probably from antelope or impala.

Kintaro knew that it would be either lions or hyenas in pursuit of their next meal.

Sure enough, his perception was proved right when he saw the sheer panic of a herd of impala leaping and sprinting in his direction, closely followed by a pack of hyenas, flanking the herd on both sides and a strategic distance behind.

Kintaro felt for his fleeing neighbours, knowing that the hyena success rate in kills was high, but he also felt he could not meddle with nature; hyenas needed to feed themselves too. *They are still disgusting animals and a constant irritant to elephants, though*, he thought.

However, this was the way of the animal world and he should not interfere.

Some of his neighbours were carnivores and some herbivores; he could not help but feel for the impala, because however quick and nimble they were, it would likely be an elder, infant, or lame individual that would fall victim.

Being hyenas, Cassaire and her pack were highly skilled when it came to feeding time, but as their leader, she had been growing more and more concerned about the incompetence of the pack – in particular her lower-ranked pack members, Vossler, Zul, Drach, Tidas, and Mortas.

Each of them had their failings. Vossler was far too gung-ho and would never wait for a command. Zul, so forgetful, he sometimes forgot to breathe! As for Drach, he was the noisiest screeching howling hyena anyone could ever have the misfortune to meet and just could not keep quiet. Tidas was completely accident prone and was keen to tell everyone that he should be in a hospital. Then there was Mortas, the scaredy-cat, always trying to run away from his own shadow.

Cassaire's strategy for the kill had been decided beforehand and they agreed that a junior impala would do for now and that it was Vossler's and Drach's task to try and prise one away from the herd. Mortas and Tidas would get ahead and then shepherd it away, rendering the defenceless creature with nowhere to go and free from the protection its family offered.

No point in giving Zul an instruction – he would only forget it, Cassaire thought.

As the plot unfolded and the chilling scene grew closer to Kintaro, he realised that the ensuing melee was heading straight for his position. He was not concerned about the speed and agility of the impala and their ability to avoid him in their frantic escape, nor was he threatened by some scrawny, bullying mongrels, picking out a defenceless animal. *After all*, he thought, *hyenas can survive on the remnants of kills other predators have left, even scavenging and cleaning up bones.*

Sure enough, the hyenas' plan was working and the cackling dogs had manoeuvred Tidas and a reluctant

Mortas into a position whereby they engineered getting themselves between the herd and one unsuspecting juvenile impala. They forced it to change direction and flee to the right of the path the rest of the herd was taking. It was then the turn of Vossler and Drach as their tiring colleagues slowed to a jogging pace, but still in the hunt.

Kintaro could see exactly what was happening and the pack strategy unfolding; however, as the two lower-ranked officers raced towards their victim and the impending outcome, they were oblivious to Kintaro's presence, just as they only had eyes for their prey, racing either side of Kintaro. He allowed the young impala to get past him, then swung his mighty trunk to the left and then the right, depositing both dogs to either side of the vulnerable creature's escape route and rolling into some dense thorny vegetation.

'Get back to your family, little one, and stay close at all times,' said Kintaro, and the lucky impala regained formation and the safety of its family.

Cassaire was furious with her team. 'Idiots,' she screamed. 'How could you miss a gigantic albino elephant in your path?'

Mortas and Tidas cowered at the ferocity of Cassaire's rant.

'Honestly, boss, we were totally focused on the meal and didn't expect an elephant to get involved,' said Mortas.

'I give you one simple task and you screw it up. It's maggots and marrow for us this evening and our percentage kill ratio has taken a battering. We will be the laughing stock of the savanna kennel club,' she cried.

***

Feeling rather pleased with himself after doing his good deed for the day, Kintaro continued his trek towards the watering hole or river his senses were telling him was not far away. A few moments later, he could see and hear the Mara River in the distance and his pace quickened at the prospect of a good drink and a relaxing bath.

Kintaro entered the river via a sandy embankment, unknowingly missing a number of white eggs, each the size of a large potato. Fortunately, he had just missed trampling on a nest, but his only thought was that of quenching his thirst.

His trunk acting like an enormous straw, he revisited the water repeatedly. As he stepped further into the river to start his bathing ritual, he felt a sharp pain at the tip of his trunk. *What is that?* he thought as the pain intensified.

Kintaro let out a trumpeting cry and instinctively pulled his trunk out of the water, revealing a huge crocodile swinging from it.

He desperately tried to shake it off but even with his new-found strength was unable to free himself from its vice-like grip. To add to his predicament, he felt the same vice-like grip on each of his ankles.

Kintaro had seriously annoyed the crocs by almost obliterating their nest, which was not the cleverest thing he could have done.

While this unfortunate and painful encounter was still unfolding, and not by chance, Narok and Issun Boshi witnessed what was going on from the skies above.

'Quick, Narok, set me down. I must help,' said Bosh.

'Are you sure, Issun?' said Narok.

'Absolutely,' said Bosh. 'Get me close.'

Narok glided down close to the commotion and Issun Boshi leapt off the eagle and landed on Kintaro's huge head. 'Don't worry, big feller, I'm here now – it looks like you need some help,' he said.

Kintaro, still struggling with the annoying crocs, could not believe his eyes as Issun Boshi slid down his trunk in the direction of the unrelenting crocodile still attached to him.

'What in the gods' name are you and what makes you think you're going to be of use to me? I don't even know what you are, and I can barely hear you,' said Kintaro.

'Charming,' Issun replied. 'You'll see how I can help.' As Issun reached the end of the elephant's trunk, he jumped onto the short rounded snout of the crocodile, brandishing his ivory needle. With tremendous precision and agility, he directed it into the left eye of the crocodile.

Instinctively and in excruciating pain, the crocodile released Kintaro, but propelled Issun high into the air; Bosh descended, as if in slow motion, straight towards the mouth of another crocodile, jaws already wide open to receive his prize. Bosh fell straight inside the reptile's mouth, no doubt gone forever.

Kintaro was dumbfounded, having now realised that

it was a tiny, perfectly formed elephant who had performed heroics and ultimately freed him from the stubborn crocodile. He then had to try and defend himself against three or more other angry crocs that believed they could dine out on him for a month.

Moments after the croc had swallowed Issun, it exploded into thousands of tiny crocodile fragments and revealed a full-sized bull elephant brandishing an ivory needle and covered in crocodile blood. Issun had stabbed the croc from within and the transformation he had experienced at home defending the chacma baboons had occurred once more, delivering Issun to his full-grown state.

'Well, come on then, big feller, let's teach these scaly lizards a lesson,' said Bosh.

'Don't tell me … you have met our friend Narok?' Kintaro said.

'Indeed I have,' said Bosh, and the two formidable bull elephants quickly disposed of the flagging crocs, slinging them out of the river one by one.

Having reached the safety of the other side of the river, Issun Boshi shook trunks with Kintaro and slowly reduced in size now that the drama was over.

'No prizes for guessing what your special talent is. But what's your name, little feller?' Kintaro asked.

'My name is Issun Boshi and one day I will tell you my story, but something tells me we were destined to meet here today. What is your name?'

By this time Issun had shrunk to his diminutive size

and Kintaro carefully scooped him up on his trunk so he could see and hear him clearly. 'My name is Kintaro and I am indebted to you for helping me. Both of us have had the pleasure of meeting Narok and I guess we are part of the plan to form his four Heavenly Kings.'

'Seems that way, big feller,' said Bosh.

'Please, call me Kintaro.'

'Okay, big feller,' said Bosh jokingly.

Kintaro placed Issun onto his head and the two new friends continued their journey, realising it was inevitable that they would meet the other two members of the Tamonten Tusks soon; they tried to guess what their special powers would be.

7

How Nakano met Yuki (Onna)

A whole lot of trouble

Readjusting to life in the wild again was not going to be easy for Nakano. Being kept in captivity for such a long time had deprived her of basic and vital lessons she would have normally been taught by her family. However, she had learned some skills from friends at the park, namely self-defence tricks passed on by Monty, plus the new-found ability Narok had bestowed upon her. That one, especially, made her feel a little weird as she tried to come to terms with what she could do with it.

When and how was she supposed to use it to help others?

These were a few of the thoughts rushing through her head as she trekked through the plains taking in the natural beauty all around her. Ever since she had been released back into the wild, the prospect of what to do next had been constantly on her mind. Knowing that

Narok had some sort of a plan for her, should she try and find her childhood family or maybe look to join another herd?

All these quandaries she had time to contemplate on her long walk back to what she imagined would become home.

Will I see Narok again and will he tell me what I should do? I hate not knowing and feel alone. I even miss the gibbering nonsense Boots used to annoy me with, she thought.

***

Meanwhile, Yuki was in the same predicament as Nakano, wandering alone among the shrubs and grasses, weaving in and out of the acacia trees and occasionally stopping for food. It hadn't been long since she had disappeared in front of her herd and hopefully demonstrated that she had a purpose in life that was different from theirs.

Unlike Nakano, Yuki was optimistic and naturally quite spiritual. She believed that fate would determine her role in life and took comfort in the knowledge that the gods would be watching over her. For now, she would continue following her instincts and basking in the sights and sounds of the wind, leaves, birds, and insects, all synchronised like members of an orchestra.

It was the dry season and many of the grasses had turned brown to conserve water. The sparse acacia trees stood like sentries standing guard. Their small waxy leaves and thorns provided much-needed food for not only elephants but giraffes and zebras. Despite the acacias suffering damage from the hungry animals, the trees cleverly combated this by allying with biting ants. The ants would settle on the trees' hungry visitors and cause discomfort. Recompense for the ants was to feast on the trees' sugary exterior.

The terrain Yuki was now trampling was cracked as it usually was in the dry season. The soil was red as plant roots found it difficult to penetrate the hardpan, restricting the growth of vegetation.

The bric-a-brac of sticks and branches was charcoal after the fires caused by lightning strikes and littered the ground, disintegrating under Yuki's feet. Still, she soldiered on until, quite unexpectedly, the sound of the familiar ground beneath her altered and the surface became unstable. Within seconds, Yuki found herself collapsing into a circular hole about the depth of a fully grown giraffe with muddy water in its base.

A cloud of dust exploded from within as the full weight of the cow elephant dropped out of sight into the horrors beneath.

As she fell, Yuki let out an almighty cry which echoed as she hit the bottom. Fortunately, she was not hurt and managed to land upright on her feet. Completely shaken and dazed, she tried to make sense of what had just happened.

It must have been an old mining hole or poacher's trap, she thought.

The remnants of broken pallets and ply board confirmed it was a trap, covered over to blend in with the surroundings. Yuki knew she was in trouble; there was little room inside and less than a metre above her. She could not see out of the trap and her trunk was the only part of her visible from above ground, waving frantically.

'Please help,' she cried, 'can anyone hear me?'

There was no one. Once the initial sounds of her fall had settled, the scene around her went back to normal.

What am I going to do, how am I going to get out of here? Yuki thought. It would not be long before nightfall and she was starting to panic. She continued waving her trunk and letting out repeated trumpeting distress calls in the hope that someone friendly would hear her. But even if they did, how would they get an elephant of her size out of this hole?

Someone or something did hear Yuki, but it sounded like the last rescue team she wanted to help her. When she took a moment to rest after continuous cries for help, she heard a haunting howl followed by several chattering, laughing cries in the distance.

This is not good, she thought.

Her suspicions were right. Rhazien the spotted hyena Issun Boshi had encountered previously was in the neighbourhood, and Rhazien could smell fear from a great distance.

One by one, Rhazien's pack edged closer to the place where Yuki was stranded. As they reached the hole about six of them circled the circumference of the pit, keeping a short distance from the edge.

Annoyingly for Yuki, they just peered down, teasing the stricken elephant, snarling and slobbering as they stood their ground.

Moments later, Yuki saw the circle of dogs part, making way for their cold-blooded leader who quietly grunted as she neared the edge.

'What have we here, boys?' she said.

'Supper,' one of her boys replied.

'More like a banquet,' she qualified. 'How did you end up in this unfortunate situation, my dear?'

'Go away, you ugly mongrel. My family will be here shortly and in numbers, so push off and leave me alone,' Yuki replied.

'Is that the family you left a short time ago, Yuki?'

'How do you know that? And how do you know my name?'

'I make it my business to know everything that goes on around here, and word is that you are the clever one in elephant circles. It will take more than brains to get you out of this mess. I also heard a mysterious tale about some hunters experiencing a full-grown elephant disappearing in front of their eyes and wrecking their camp. That wasn't you, Yuki, by any chance?' Rhazien asked.

'I don't know what you are talking about. Now do something useful for once in your life and get me some help,' said Yuki.

'The only help you will see, Yuki, is me and my friends here helping ourselves to your ample flesh, once you have perished through starvation,' Rhazien replied.

'So how do you expect to dine out on me? This hole is too deep. Even a fit evil wretch like you could not climb out of here.'

'As you know, Yuki, being so clever yourself, we hyenas are often affectionately known as the janitors of the savanna because we clean everything up, including bones. On this occasion, we will sacrifice munching on your substantial ribcage and use it as a ladder to climb out,' said Rhazien.

'You seem to have thought of everything. Everything apart from the protection I will get from the gods.'

'Will your gift of disappearing get you out of this mess, Yuki?' Rhazien asked.

As Rhazien taunted Yuki, there came a bolt out of the blue in the form of a boulder hurtling its way towards the scene, narrowly missing Yuki's waving trunk and completely taking out two of the hyenas guarding the trap.

To Rhazien's surprise, a second elephant appeared out of the sun and stood, magnificent, adjacent to where the remainder of the dogs were now hiding behind Rhazien.

It was Nakano.

'Perhaps we won't have to wait until Yuki dies, gentlemen … we have ourselves a choice on the menu, albeit one that appears to be a little feisty and has the ability to hurtle rocks. Take your positions, men, and let's opt for the à la carte on terra firma,' said Rhazien.

Nakano charged at the formidable foe, wielding her

kendo pole. The hyenas took immediate evasive action and launched at Nakano one by one, inflicting superficial but painful wounding.

Yuki could not see what was happening but heard charging calls from one of her own. 'Be careful, whoever you are,' she cried.

Yuki also heard another sound she had not expected to hear, getting louder and closer.

While Rhazien's dogs were busy fighting with Nakano, she also heard the noise getting closer. She turned around to see for herself and was bulldozed by the biggest rhino she had ever seen.

The remaining hyenas raced to Rhazien's defence to see if she was still alive and looking for guidance as to what to do next. Rhazien rose to her feet and stood in front of her team. It was a stand-off.

Ten snarling, hungry hyenas versus Nakano and Clem looking menacingly muscular and snorting profusely.

The stand-off appeared to be suspended in time while all protagonists considered their options when they were joined by a four-by-four driven by Professor Gon, who was clearly not there to act as an impartial official.

Gon smartly manoeuvred his vehicle to the side of the heroes and, instantly, the odds had changed.

He spoke out as he always did. 'Now listen here, young lady, if you know what's good for you. Run along and think yourselves lucky that we haven't taken any further action yet.'

'You may have gained an unfair advantage this time, you bunch of misfits, but you haven't seen the last of us,' Rhazien said.

The dishevelled battle-weary dogs took the cowardly option and jogged away, conceding defeat.

'How can I thank you all?' cried a voice from the pit. 'And I don't even know who you are.'

'Don't worry, madam,' Gon replied, 'what's more important is how we get you out of this blessed hole.'

Nakano, Clem, Yuki, and Gon made their introductions and swiftly exchanged ideas as to how to get Yuki out.

'Let's send for a helicopter,' Clem suggested.

'How are you going to do that, my dear friend? Do you have a radio or telephone on you by any chance?' said Gon.

'Hadn't thought of that,' Clem replied, embarrassed. 'I know, let's throw down some ladders.'

'Thank you for your suggestions, Clem, but stick to being the brawn for now,' Gon said.

'Perhaps we need to make the pit bigger so that Yuki has more room to climb out?' suggested Nakano.

'I think that's a damn good shout, my dear, but we will still need to give Yuki a helping hand,' said the prof.

'Professor Gon, does your vehicle have a winch?' Yuki asked.

'Yes it does, my dear, and it has some rope and strapping too. But how will we get the strapping around you? I still think we need something to excavate the hole, to make it more gently sloping, to help you climb out.' Gon looked at Clem and scratched his chin as if a light bulb had gone on in his head. 'You know, Clem, I have always admired your fully grown horn.'

'What are you thinking, Prof?' Clem asked in a worried tone.

'You, my friend, are the closest thing to an excavator we have right now. How are you fixed for a spot of manual labour?' Gon asked.

'You want me to dig her out on my own?' Clem replied.

'Exactly.'

'I could position the straps around Yuki's stomach,' said Nakano.

'My dear, there's hardly enough room for Yuki in there, let alone someone like you.'

'You don't understand, Professor. I can make inanimate objects move at will,' she said.

'And I can make myself disappear,' said Yuki.

'Now hold on a minute here, folks. I have been studying the animal kingdom for most of my life and I know that elephants cannot disappear or make things move. That's quite ridiculous!' said Gon.

'There's no time to explain to you now, Professor, it's getting dark and we need to get Yuki out,' said Nakano.

'Well, I'm willing to give it a go,' said Clem and immediately started breaking up the ground on one side of the pit.

It was not long before Clem's immense strength and

determination had fashioned a ramp, forming an entrance to the pit, but it was still too steep for Yuki to climb out.

Gon got back into the Land Rover and positioned the vehicle near to the entrance Clem had created, with the winch in position. He handed the straps and rope to Nakano.

'Now then, ladies, show an old expert in his field that he still has a lot to learn about elephants.'

Nakano did not touch the straps but concentrated hard. The straps rose from the ground like snakes being charmed and entered the pit.

This was the signal for Yuki to do her stuff and in an instant she disappeared, enabling Nakano to get the straps underneath her stomach and out the other side, coming to a stop just short of the Land Rover winch.

'That's unbelievable,' Gon said and tied the straps to the winch. To his amazement, Yuki then reappeared, ready for the next phase of the extraction.

Gon jumped excitedly into the four-by-four, started the engine, turned on the winch, and gradually pulled away from the hole.

It was working; the straps tightened around Yuki's stomach and she wearily moved her huge legs in the direction of the makeshift ramp. Despite some progress, however, it was clear that the four-by-four was struggling. Nakano and Clem raced towards the vehicle and pushed from behind, giving it the impetus to pull Yuki completely out of the pit.

It worked – she was pulled free.

'Thank you all so much. I thought I was going to die alone in that hole and never have the chance to fulfil my destiny,' said Yuki.

'You must tell me about this destiny thing and how you both came about your powers,' Gon said.

'Hello, Yuki,' Nakano said, offering Yuki her trunk.

'Do you think fate brought us together like this?' Yuki asked.

'Could be, or maybe Narok had something to do with it. Have you encountered the other two he spoke about?' Nakano said.

'Not yet, but hopefully when we do, it will not be as traumatic as this introduction.'

The four friends chatted for a while until Clem and Gon headed off to leave Yuki and her new partner knowing that the next phase of their quest would be to meet up at some point with the others, to continue their adventure.

8

Boys meet the Girls

To solve poaching, the first thing you need to do is
to solve poverty

Kingsley, the park ranger, was apprehensive today because sightings of poachers were on the increase and instances of retaliation threatened the safety of his men, who were made up mostly of locals looking for work to help feed their families.

They understood their role, which was to protect an area rich in biodiversity, such as the Tarangire National Park, often risking their lives.

He had done his best to train his team as much as he could, but declines in funding had meant the reduction of professional training, especially relating to firearms, crucial for the role in the modern bush.

As well as being liked by his men, Kingsley was also well respected. He tried to impart as much of the knowledge he had learnt for his diploma at the African Field Ranger Training Service, which he was fortunate to be awarded on a scholarship funded by an anonymous benefactor.

Having lived most of his earlier years in the port of Mombasa, it was his interest and love of animals that drove his ambition to contribute what he could to the preservation of endangered species. Hence he studied hard at school and college to fulfil that dream. Kingsley was also proud of his national diploma in Nature Conservation and had fond and proud memories of his first day at work ten years ago in neighbouring Tanzania, dressed in a khaki uniform, dark green beret, and shiny black boots, a uniform he had been proud to wear ever since.

***

Today was similar to most other days, in that his team would rise at five in the morning to check their equipment and utility belt, which would contain a flask, knife, and fully charged cell phone. He requested that his men gather around the country's flag at five thirty for a bugle call where everyone saluted, standing to attention. This gave them a tremendous feeling of patriotism and significance.

Their shift was to be a three-day patrol in a pickup truck with six of his men, each assigned a specific responsibility, taking charge of firearms, ammunition, driving, cooking, radio, and fuel.

The firearms were individually numbered and assigned to a specific ranger and the ammunition was allocated carefully because it was generally in short supply. The firearms were old Soviet AK47 assault rifles and prone to failing.

Axes and machetes were also standard issue; they were needed sometimes to clear tracks of trees uprooted by elephants.

Before leaving at 7 a.m., Kingsley gave out the itinerary for the patrol and the location where they would set up camp. This was not revealed beforehand to avoid leakage and potential ambush.

'Okay, men, let's do our bit,' he ordered, and the pickup truck headed off into the bush.

Some thirty minutes into the patrol, Kingsley stood up on the pickup truck, giving him a good vantage point, to look out for evidence of human activity in the bush. A campfire smoking or vultures circling could indicate the position of a recent kill by lions or hyenas, but sometimes by poachers. However, poachers had recently recognised that vultures could alert the authorities as to their whereabouts and had even taken to poisoning carcasses with chemicals, thereby killing the vultures and reducing their numbers dramatically.

By nine thirty the patrol had already discovered some vulture activity and investigated further. They encountered a rhino carcass among some long grasses. The stricken animal had been shot a couple of days ago by poachers and its horn removed for so-called medicines.

'Take a picture and mark the location with the GPS,' said Kingsley to one of his men.

They conducted a forensic search of the area looking for clues, but only came across a plastic bag, which they handled carefully using a stick to ensure it did not contain a trap that could severe the hand of a ranger.

Having recorded the incident, the patrol continued on its scheduled patrol and stopped for lunch at precisely one o'clock.

By this time, it was blisteringly hot, so lunch was a quick break, taking in sandwiches and water. It would not be long before they were on route again, hoping that the poachers responsible for the rhino killing would still be in the vicinity.

***

As the rangers continued on their patrol, Nakano and Yuki were steadily making their way in the bush. They chatted about the sequence of events that had led them to their encounter with Narok and eventually meeting each other.

'I had no idea what was going to happen to me until I met that crazy eagle,' said Nakano, referring to her experience on the ship home.

'Narok is not crazy,' said Yuki, 'he has a plan for us all in a much greater undertaking. This will become apparent very soon, I'm sure.'

'You seem to come out with such wise words, Yuki. You are far more level-headed than me.'

'But you have qualities too, Nakano, and you use your newly found talent very wisely. You are more streetwise than I,' Yuki replied.

'When do you think we will meet the others? Do you

think they will be girls too?' asked Nakano.

'I don't think it will be long now. As for the gender of our soon-to-be compatriots, I have no idea. If they are boys, I would be more concerned about them pulling their weight,' Yuki pointed out.

'What abilities do you think Narok has given them, Yuki?'

'If they're boys, I hope it's deodorant and good manners.'

Nakano laughed and the two elephants continued on their way in anticipation of meeting the others.

***

At the same time, Kintaro and Issun, who was seated on top of Kintaro's head, were unknowingly wandering towards the girls from the opposite direction.

'Where are we going, big feller? I'm getting sore perched here on top of your bony scalp?'

'Think yourself lucky, shorty, it's me doing all the leg work. Now be quiet and stop itching my head,' Kintaro said.

'Do you know where we're going or are you just winging it?' asked Bosh.

'I'm looking for a sign,' said Kintaro.

'A sign?' said Bosh. 'This is not Serengeti-this-way, you lump.'

'A sign from Narok, you little—'

'Now then, big feller, is the heat getting to you?' said Bosh.

'Narok will give us a sign,' said Kintaro. 'Everything that has happened so far seems to have been for good reason. So be patient, shut up, and help me keep a lookout for him, up above.'

'Narok said there are four heavenly kings. We are two of them. When do you think we'll meet the other two?' asked Bosh, even though he was supposed to be being quiet.

'I have no idea, but I'm sure that when the time is right, we will get to meet them.'

'You are so boring, big feller. Do you think they will be girls – and attractive girls too?'

'What has that got to do with anything, Issun? We have a job to do and no time for teenage shenanigans,' Kintaro replied.

'Yeah, but—'

'There's no *yeah, but* about it. Now keep your eyes open.'

It was not long before Kintaro's faith in Narok was confirmed when they caught sight of the eagle flying above them and indicating that they should follow him, which they gladly did.

***

Kingsley's patrol had all but finished their first day's watch and were heading towards the area they had designated to set up camp for the night. It would be dark by six thirty, which left them one hour to find the spot to set up their tents and light a fire to ward off the odd lion or hyena.

As they drove, Kingsley felt uneasy; there was very little sound apart from that of the pickup. Normally he would hear cicadas and chirping crickets, buffalo or lion calls, but it was deadly quiet.

'Something is not right,' he said to his men. All six of them raised their rifles, forming a lookout in all directions. Suddenly there was a bang – it sounded like one of the tyres had suffered a blowout. The driver started to lose control and the vehicle swerved from side to side, narrowly missing kopjes and trees.

Kingsley knew it was not a blowout. Someone had shot at the front wheel – they were under attack. 'Stop the vehicle!' he shouted. The pickup skidded to a halt in a small clearing about fifty metres from where they had first been shot at.

'Get out of the truck,' he ordered, and his men quickly exited the pickup and took up position, crouched behind it. Then the bullets started to rain on them. 'We are under attack. It's poachers,' he shouted, 'return fire.'

The rangers returned fire on their assailants but had no idea where they were. From the sheer volume of rounds that were deposited on them, Kingsley knew that they were outnumbered.

He was right; in among the protection offered by the long grasses, trees, and shrubs, the poachers were dug in, led by their notorious leader, Yamauba. Standing at six foot six tall, Yamauba was an intimidating man. He was of Afrikaans origin and spoke in a distinct African Dutch accent; he was dressed in typical apparel suitable for the climate – beige shirt with upturned collar, white T-shirt beneath, black combat trousers – and had short greased black hair, a pencil-thin moustache, and dark brown eyes. He carried a Czechoslovakian CZ550 with .375 calibre round, capable of bringing down big game.

His poachers were also armed with the same weaponry, which had no doubt been smuggled into Tanzania, exploiting lax gun regulations and government corruption.

Kingsley feared for his men's lives as one of them took a gunshot to the shoulder, reducing their defences to five.

'Stay down, men,' he ordered; their AK47s were no match for the opposition. 'Radio for backup.'

Yamauba ordered his men to split up, with military precision. Two groups of three men manoeuvred their way to attack Kingsley's patrol from either side.

***

Kintaro, Issun, Nakano, and Yuki heard the gunfire and raced to the scene from opposite directions. First to arrive at the gunfight and the rangers' position were Nakano and Yuki. Nakano immediately saw the threat from the rangers' right and saw the poachers open fire before the patrol had time to react and defend themselves.

'Look – to the right,' said Kingsley, but it was too late – the poachers had already let out a burst of shots in their direction.

Nakano sprang into action and focused, using her power to divert the path of the poachers' rounds away from the rangers.

Just before hitting their intended targets, the poachers' bullets curved to the left and right, missing them.

'Missed,' Nakano shouted excitedly at the outcome.

But how was she going to help defuse any subsequent attempts? She had to do something; she realised the patrol would be subject to more gunfire from the right.

She spotted a young black mamba snake about the length of a Maasai spear and one of the most poisonous in Africa, minding its own business on a nearby kopje, and imagined the panic if it landed in the vicinity of the poachers before they had a chance to reload.

To the mamba's surprise, it levitated from the kopje and effortlessly floated in the direction of the poachers, coming to rest gently at their feet. Terror set in among the poachers when they realised a mamba was among them, whose bite could kill a man in a matter of hours.

Yamauba heard the screams of his men from a distance then saw them fleeing for their lives into the bush.

Meanwhile, as Nakano was dealing with the threat to the patrol from the right, Yuki was conscious of the attack from the left. *What can I do?* she thought; she didn't possess the same power as Nakano.

The only thing Yuki could do was disappear and that was exactly what she did. In her invisible state, she made her way towards the threat from the left and positioned herself in great danger in front of the poachers. Only then did she reappear, much to the dismay of the attackers, who believed that the devil himself had confronted them.

With evil spirits at large, the poachers mirrored the actions of their colleagues to the right and fled the scene in panic and fear of satanic retribution.

The heroics of the girls were only part of the battle – there was also the threat from Yamauba, whose men still outnumbered the patrol. He also had a few tricks up his sleeve.

This was the moment when Kintaro and the diminutive Issun Boshi needed to spring into action.

Despite the welcome support the boys offered, Kingsley and his men kept firing at their foe, careful not to target their aim at the elephants.

Bosh revelled in the prospect of combat and slid down Kintaro's trunk straight into a box of grenades that Yamauba was reaching for.

'Too late,' shouted Bosh as he slammed his needle against the bottom of the wooden box and instantly grew to full size, scattering the ammunition in all directions.

As Yamauba's men turned their sights on to Issun, Kintaro bulldozed his way through their formation, swatting them like flies and careering into one of their four-by-fours, squashing it into a lump of metal.

Yamauba was in shock, to say the least; with all his firepower and guile, he had been thwarted by a foe he least expected and escaped by the skin of his teeth in the only four-by-four still operational.

Once the threat was over and Yamauba and his men

defeated, the four braves found themselves facing each other for the first time. None of them knew who should speak first, or what to say until Kingsley and his men approached them.

'I had heard the stories, but never truly believed them – you guys are for real and we cannot thank you enough,' said Kingsley.

'No thanks needed, Ranger. We are all fighting the same battle and that is clear to us now,' said Kintaro.

'Thank you again and may the savannah gods be always with you.'

Kingsley and his men continued on their way, with the understanding suggested by their leader that what had been witnessed today should always remain their secret.

'Okay … this is awkward,' said Bosh. 'I guess you two make up Narok's four heavenly kings, alongside the big feller and me, of course.' He was gradually reducing in size before their eyes.

'Now we can see what Narok saw in you, little one. Where have you gone?' Yuki said.

'Oh, I'm still here,' said Bosh, 'but good things come in small packages.' This was a familiar line from him now. Kintaro offered his friend his trunk and Issun Boshi scampered up to take his place on his borrowed throne.

'It's a pleasure to meet you, ladies. My name is Kintaro and this little chap is Issun Boshi, or Bosh to us.'

Yuki was the first of the girls to speak. 'We are pleased to finally meet the other half of our ensemble too, Kintaro. My name is Yuki-Onna and this is Nakano. We knew from Narok that our paths would cross eventually and, after this encounter, we now know the special powers he has entrusted to you.'

'Great, now that the introductions are over – have you got a boyfriend, Nakano?' said Bosh.

'If I did, Bosh, he would look nothing like you!' Nakano replied sternly.

'Only asking,' said Bosh, not in the least deterred by Nakano's rebuke.

After the introductions and initial banter, the four new friends continued to get to know each other, long into the night.

Ultimately, there would be a goal, but it was acknowledged that there could be many more adventures before they fulfilled their destiny.

9

Mogwai

Monster or evil spirit

Yamauba had plenty of time, on his long journey back to Mombasa, to think about how he was going to explain the extraordinary events of the day before to his boss.

Mogwai will not believe me, he thought. *How am I going to explain losing my men, vehicles, and weaponry, but most of all the stash of ivory and horns we had accumulated over the last four days? He will be furious – he had deadlines to meet and clients to satisfy.*

Yamauba was a tough guy, but the threat of retribution from Mogwai did not bear thinking about. How was he going to explain that his failure to ambush a ranger patrol was down to the interference of four elephants?

Oh, and by the way, they all seemed to have special powers too. Yeah, right! he contemplated. *Perhaps I should cut and run.* But he knew Mogwai would find him and punish him. *Anyway, Yamauba doesn't run from anybody*, he reminded himself.

'My grandfather fought in the Second Boer War against the British, my father was a mercenary, and I am ex-Recces Special Forces. To hell with him!' he shouted out loud.

Having given himself a stern talking to, Yamauba eventually pulled up outside the Shanghai Garden restaurant, which Mogwai owned, mainly as a front for his dodgy dealings. Despite his predicament, Yamauba still managed to chuckle to himself about the name, because in slang terms, to Shanghai someone was to trick them into working for you.

The restaurant was situated on Diana Road, opposite the Diana Reef Hotel, and typically cooked authentic Cantonese food served on lazy-Susan tables.

He made his way indoors, past an extravagant exotic aquarium and through a beaded curtain door, to be greeted on the other side by one of Mogwai's henchmen, who was armed with an automatic rifle, the butt end next to his right shoulder and pointing downwards. The man ushered Yamauba towards an adjacent door and opened it for him.

Mogwai's office was quite small, considering his ill-gotten wealth, with no windows, a table at the far end opposite the door, and a filing cabinet to the left of the desk. Yamauba could not help but notice he had armed guards in all four corners of the room.

In front of the desk was a single chair, not upholstered but of weathered wooden construction, which looked as though it might collapse if excess weight were placed upon it.

'Come in, my friend,' said Mogwai, 'sit down and make yourself at home.'

The boss sat at the business end of the desk smoking a cigar and clasping a small Chinese cup of tea.

Yamauba obeyed yet another command from a spurious officer of sorts and sat uncomfortably in a chair that wasn't made for a man of his size.

Mogwai, by comparison, was a slight figure, obviously of Chinese descent, clean-shaven and dressed in slacks, a black T-shirt, and a white linen jacket.

His face was pitted as if he had suffered acute acne in adolescence, and he was balding, apart from above his ears and under his crown.

***

Mogwai had grown up in Xinjiang in north-eastern China, where his father was an opium dealer and counterfeiter, meaning that he wanted for nothing as a child due to his father's questionable income. As a child he was never out of trouble at school and was renowned for his cruelty towards animals. This was topped by him selling the family dog to the local market for dog meat. He never revealed the true outcome of the family pet's fate to his parents.

When he was sixteen, the family moved to Beijing, where his father developed his villainous career by expanding into internet fraud, involving credit cards and identity sales. Mogwai inherited some of his father's entrepreneurial skills, and enrolled at college and university to learn languages, including English, French, Russian, Arabic, and Swahili, and became fluent in all.

Having once secured a school trip to Kenya, Mogwai saw for himself the opportunities in Africa, with the demand for ivory spearheading an ambition to get rich and quick. Back in Beijing, he had seen the specialist shops selling intricate ivory carvings, such as temples and chess sets. More important to him was the price people were prepared to pay for such pieces of art with absolutely no remorse about where they came from.

After working in his father's business for ten years, learning the ropes of illegal trade, Mogwai decided that he wanted to take advantage of his language skills and secured a role in Kenya as an interpreter. His position gave him access to many documents from government officials, which afforded him valuable insight into how easy corruption was and who was getting very wealthy out of it.

This role also proved worthwhile when he needed contacts for his main enterprise, which was the poaching of ivory tusks from elephants and horns from rhinos.

Although sales in China had been prohibited, procurement only allowed with a permit, some ivory was still getting through on the black market. This did not deter him, and he soon realised new markets in Thailand, Hong Kong, Vietnam, and Laos.

Having established himself as one of the main ivory traffickers in Africa by the age of thirty, Mogwai further enhanced his portfolio by securing the distribution rights

of aviation and marine fuel outside Kenya and into Dar
Es Salaam in Tanzania.

He then formed his first semi-legal company called
GasCom Tanzania Ltd with no public outcry relating to
bribery and corruption.

***

'Tell me, Yama, why are you here? I did not expect you
back so soon,' said Mogwai.

'My name is Yamauba.'

'I apologise, Yarpie,' which Yamauba knew meant
farm boy, 'I should mind my manners when speaking to
an employee with such a pedigree as yours. So tell me why
someone as highly skilled as you should return to me
empty-handed, without his men and equipment?'

'How do you know that I have returned with
nothing?' Yamauba asked.

Mogwai took another sip of his tea then once again
turned his attention to Yamauba. 'I know everything,
Yama. I make it my business to know things even before
they happen.'

'We were ambushed.'

'Oh, I apologise. I thought it was you doing the
ambushing?' said Mogwai.

'We were, but then we were ambushed.'

'Ambushed by who?' Mogwai asked.

'Elephants.'

'Elephants?'

'Yes, four elephants with special powers,' said

Yamauba with a straight face.

'What sort of special powers?'

'You tell me, you know everything before it happens,' Yamauba said sarcastically.

'Enough!' said Mogwai and thumped the desk, causing the four armed guards to ready their weapons and point them in Yamauba's direction. 'If this is true, I will overlook your inadequacies on this occasion. Providing you bring me at least one of these *special* elephants alive. This, I have to see. I have just the client who would pay handsomely for such a possession.'

'I will need more men, transport, cages, tranquilisers and time if you want me to capture one alive.'

Mogwai paused and took a puff from his cigar. 'The first four on your list I can give you, the time I cannot. Now get out of my sight.'

Yamauba rose from the chair and left the room with his life still intact.

He had a new mission in front of him and very little time in which to succeed. Failure now was not an option.

10

Maake

Dare to be king

Nakano liked to take herself off and away from the others for a bit of 'me time', taking in the sights and sounds of the environment she was now living in.

It was usually early evening when the temperatures were still very high and the bush was generally quiet. This gave her the chance to remember the time when she was very young – and to get acquainted with life in the bush, as an adult.

Of all her senses, the one she appreciated the most was hearing, and she was becoming more and more adept at identifying the sounds various animals made. Cicadas and crickets were a given, but the orchestral tones of her fellow elephants trumpeting to their hearts' content and their growls reminded her of a rickety old motorbike one of the safari park staff used to get around.

Baboons who barked like dogs, letting you know they were there.

Frogs croaked like creaking doors and hippos grunted

like fat men snoring.

These were all familiar tunes from the savanna. She remembered hearing other animal sounds when she was very young. The sound of impalas snorting like pigs when rutting, leopard calls like a saw cutting through wood and hyenas laughing at their own jokes.

All of them will ultimately sleep under the stars on this magical planet we take so much for granted, she thought.

The dusk chorus was about to be disturbed.

The nearby familiar sounds died down and an air of uneasiness once again commanded all her other senses.

A flock of lilac-breasted roller birds raised the alarm with their distinctive guttural *rak rak* cries as they exited the termite nest they were feeding on.

She could now hear a different, more daunting resonance – a huffing, snorting sound, which seemed to be getting closer. She instinctively knew she was in danger and her suspicions were confirmed. Slowly emerging from the long grasses was a full-grown male lion with a blackish-brown mane and a branding iron symbol on his right hind leg.

His name was Maake and it was rumoured that he had been captured by a Russian circus and forced to fight another lion to the death for a gambling ring. Maake's owner had branded him with the 'Dare to be King' symbol to make him even more aggressive before the fight.

He was the most feared lion in all Africa.

Maake was reputed to be the ultimate hunter in bush-life history, often bringing down full-grown elephants on his own, when normally it would take two lions at the very least. The tactic was always to attack from the elephant's rear and lunge onto its back, bringing it down and avoiding the trunk and tusks at the front.

What would he want with me? There must be easier prey if he's hungry, she thought.

But food was not what the lion was looking for. Maake prowled around her like he was weighing up his options, then he started to speak in a fiendishly menacing tone.

'So which one are you?' he asked.

'What do you mean?' Nakano replied, holding her kendo pole in readiness for an attack.

'You know what I mean,' he replied. 'I have heard about the four heavenly kings or Tamonten Tusks on the bush telegraph, but didn't believe it. I had to come and see for myself.'

'Look, Mr Lion,' said Nakano.

'My name is Maake,' he replied, 'everyone around here knows my name.'

'Apologies, Maake, but we have no quarrel with you, I can assure you.'

'Oh, but you do. Word is that you possess special powers and can defeat anyone and anything,' he replied. 'So what's your special power threatening my position here?'

'I don't want any trouble with you, sir, so please leave me alone and no one will get hurt.'

'I guess I'll just have to find out for myself then.' He leapt at Nakano like a sprinter out of the blocks.

Nakano needed her power more than ever; she focused her gaze on the lion's lunge and used her new-found power to deflect his initial attack away from her. He landed on his feet a safe distance away.

'Oh, I get it now,' he said, 'you're the one who can make things move on their own. My understanding is that you can only defend yourself for a limited period though. Prepare to fall victim to the one who would Dare to be King.'

Maake promptly launched another vicious attack on Nakano, and this time he was hit by a rock on the side of his enormous jaw. This dazed him, but he collected himself and stalked Nakano, turning left, then right, and left again in front of her, weighing up his next move.

Nakano knew that cries for help would not be heard and she prepared herself for yet another onslaught. The lion lunged towards her again and she instinctively whipped up dust from the ground and directed it towards his eyes, temporarily blinding him.

However, this did not deter Maake. He let out a ferocious growl and circled for yet another strike, knowing that her evasive measures could not last.

Nakano could feel her power gradually diminishing and accepted that soon she would only have her trusty pole to defend herself. She watched Maake positioning himself for what would be his moment of triumph. He thrust his muscular frame towards her.

Then from out of nowhere another full-grown lion burst through the bushes, leapt into the air as if in slow motion and grappled with Maake in the nick of time.

It was Boots.

The two battling lions hit the ground, clasping each other, and fought ferociously as if challenging for pack leader.

Nakano was stunned by the severity of the fight and feared for her friend's life – Maake was getting the better of him. The combatants were now facing each other on hind legs and trading slaps, inflicting wounds with each blow.

Boots was starting to tire, but Maake kept administering blow after blow.

As far as Maake was concerned, this was to the death. Just as he was about to administer the fatal blow on poor Boots, Kintaro burst through the long grasses, immediately identifying the bad guy on top of Boots.

Head down, Kintaro butted Maake in the midriff and sent him hurtling towards a nearby tree.

Winded and now outnumbered, Maake conceded that this time his fight was over. 'So you must be Kintaro?' he said in a higher-pitched voice than normal.

'I am. Now find that rock you came from under and leave while you still can,' Kintaro replied.

'You haven't seen the last of me, Kintaro, so keep your tough elephant wits about you.' Maake limped off back into the bush.

Boots was still lying on the ground, licking his

wounds and lucky to be alive. Nakano comforted him. 'I see you still have some Monty tricks up your sleeve, Boots,' she said.

'Not enough,' Boots replied. 'That cat is a killer and would have finished me off if your friend hadn't arrived.'

'Well, I think you're a hero and I cannot thank you enough for saving me.'

'Are you okay, brave lion?' Kintaro asked.

'Yes, just a few scratches, but hey, I can now say that I took on the great Maake and survived, can't I?' replied Boots.

'You sure can, my friend. Here, let me help you up,' said Kintaro, offering Boots his trunk, helping him to his feet.

'Come and meet the others,' said Nakano.

'Okay,' said Boots, 'only for a short while though. I have to get back to my pack.'

'You have a pack?' asked Nakano.

The catch-up conversation continued as the three made their way back to meet the others.

11

Dr Max

Philanthropist and conservationist

'Tell me again why we're meeting some bloke from Vermany?' said Clem, who was jogging alongside the professor's four-by-four.

Gon and Clem were making their way to the Tarangire National Park.

'Clem, my dear friend, it's not Vermany. He's from Germany, which is an extremely important country in Europe. The *bloke* you are referring to is a gentleman making a real difference with his philanthropic efforts to conserve the future of endangered species, especially elephants.'

'So he plays orchestral music to elephants then?' Clem asked.

'No, not philharmonic, philanthropic, as in charitable,' Gon replied.

'So he's irritable but musical and likes elephants?'

'Nooo,' Gon said, 'you're irritating me now. He is a very successful businessman, who donates much of his wealth to the conservation of endangered species such as your own.'

'Why do you use such big words, Prof? I'm just a rhino. Blessed, I know, in terms of my strength and drop-dead good looks, but unfortunately not in the brains department.'

'Good looks, my dear fellow? Where did you get that from?'

'By the way,' said Clem, 'I thought you said he was only interested in elephants and not the black rhino. So how can he help me?'

'His passion is the plight of elephants, yes,' Gon replied, 'but Dr Max is just one of many like-minded individuals who care about rhinos too and all other threatened species. He not only cares about animals but plant life too. That's why we're meeting with him today.'

'Dr Max?' Clem said. 'Isn't that a sugar-cane drink from a can that some safari goers selfishly leave behind? Did he make his money out selling cans of soda?'

'No, Clem. Are you purposely trying to annoy me today?' Gon asked. Would you like me to explain to you who Dr Maximilian Schwarz is?'

'Yes please, Prof. Do you think he will have some free soda samples with him?'

'Will you be serious for once and listen?' said Gon.

Gon went on to explain to Clem that Dr Max had studied hard at university in Germany and America where he gained his degree in engineering and later made his money in construction, forming his own company.

'Today he is a very wealthy man who leaves the running of his company to others and focuses all his time, dedication and most of his wealth on wildlife, climate change, and the survival of our planet.'

'He sounds like a barrel of laughs, can't wait to meet him,' said Clem, 'but all his money hasn't helped the decline in black rhino and elephant numbers so far.'

'It will, Clem, have patience. Dr Max has already donated millions of dollars in stem cell science and hybrid embryonic technology to try and save the northern white rhino, where only two females remain in the entire world. He is just one member of a group of delegates from many of the world's countries attending a convention in Nairobi next month, to tackle such issues as extinction, poaching, and hunting,' said Gon.

'How often does this convention happen, Prof?'

'Every three years, and usually key decisions are made during the last two days relating to law-making, they are so important.'

***

It was mid-afternoon when Gon and Clem arrived at the office of the Chief Park Warden in Arusha, Tanzania. They were greeted by Dr Max and park ranger Kingsley, who had deputised for the Chief Park Warden of the Tarangire National Park.

'How are you, my dear friend,' said Dr Max, hugging the professor, 'and who is this friend of yours?'

'I'm very well, Dr Max. It's so good to see you again.

The last time we met was in London three years ago at the convention. We have so much to catch up on.'

'Err, hum,' said Clem, coughing as if to attract attention, 'the doctor asked who I was, Prof.'

'I do apologise. This is Clem, my assistant,' said Gon.

'Your assistant!' Clem said.

'I am very pleased to make your acquaintance, Clem. Come now, let's have some tea and we can chat awhile,' said Dr Max.

Maximillian Schwarz was a distinguished and handsome mature gentleman with a generous flock of silver-grey hair and a well-established beard. He was dressed in beige trousers, brown boots, and an expensive-looking white linen shirt, unbuttoned to reveal his upper chest hair, which matched the hair on his head.

Kingsley went to the kitchen to prepare the refreshments and Clem lay down beside the two friends, who were now seated at a wooden picnic table in front of the office and shaded by a canopy.

Gon and Dr Max chatted for some time, covering the issues on the agenda for the convention. Given that there were fifty-six items on the last agenda three years ago, there was a lot to get through, including climate change, the ivory trade, hunting permits, tourism, not forgetting conservation, and many other topics.

'No doubt the UNEO, IFAW, CITIES, IUCN and the WWF will all have contributions to add,' said Dr Max.

Kingsley returned a short time later with the

refreshments and some cake his wife Lauren had baked that morning.

'One thing we have not discussed, though, is security,' Gon said.

'Good point, my friend. We will have some very important delegates at the convention, including leaders of countries. Ramping up security will be of paramount importance, given the threat of criminal activities.'

Kingsley entered the conversation. Security was something he knew about and he was quick to mention increased poacher attacks on his patrols. 'They are happening regularly now,' he said.

'I was shocked to hear about the attack on your patrol, Kingsley,' said Dr Max, 'it seemed as though it was a planned attack, but was apparently foiled by some elephant assistance?'

'Yes, it's true,' said Kingsley, turning to Professor Gon. 'We would not have survived without their intervention. I had promised to keep the elephants a secret, but it seems that everyone has now heard about these heroic animals.'

'That's interesting, Kingsley. I think Clem and I have already met two of them. Does one have very distinctive tattoos? The other elephant disappeared in front of our eyes. I heard about your incident on my travels. Some locals seemed to exaggerate the story, claiming that these elephants had very special powers. This now makes sense. The two elephants we met must be part of the group of four they call the Tamonten Tusks.'

'They are not exaggerating, Professor. It's true, there were four of them. Each used their powers to outwit the poachers and help us,' said Kingsley.

'What powers do the others possess?' said Gon.

'I cannot say for sure, I can only tell you what I saw.'

'What exactly did you see?' asked Dr Max.

'I saw heroic acts, ranging from unspeakable strength to invisibility, and objects, bullets even, being diverted away from us. Most definitely saving our lives,' said Kingsley.

'Extraordinary,' said Gon, 'there is no scientific evidence to corroborate elephants having individual powers, other than the instincts and abilities they naturally possess. I would love to know what the fourth special power is.'

The group continued with their meeting and pondered whether they would encounter the special elephants in the future.

12

Taken ...

Kamikakushi

The Tamonten Tusks were still full of the euphoria of helping Kingsley during the ambush, and excited about being able to put their newly acquired skills to the test.

'You were great!' Bosh said to Nakano.

'No, you were great,' she replied.

'No, you were so much better than me, Naki.'

'Don't call me Naki,' she replied, 'and yes, okay, I was so much better than you,' she joked.

Listening to the banter, Kintaro felt that he needed to intervene. 'Now, now, children. Narok gave us our powers to do good things, and certainly not to benefit us in any shape or form. Forgive the pun, Nakano.'

'Sorry, you are right. It's him being childish.' Nakano indicated Bosh.

'No offence taken, big feller,' said Bosh, 'but I was amazing.'

Yuki entered the conversation in a sensible, motherly

tone. 'Okay, everyone, let's stop the back-slapping and get to our next destination.'

***

'Where are we going?' asked Bosh as they made their way across the plains.

Clouds started to obscure the blue skies above and the temperature dropped significantly. Impalas and zebras seemed to sense a change in the weather and were vacating the area as if expecting some disturbance to their grazing.

'Can you guys feel the winds picking up?' said Nakano.

'Yes, I have noticed the wind,' said Yuki. 'It feels a little cooler too.'

'We're making our way to the Burungi Lake where we can freshen up and take in some water, no doubt alongside some disgusting warthogs,' said Kintaro.

'Did you know that the Tarangire means river of warthogs?' said Yuki.

'Thank you, Yuki, I'll sleep better tonight after knowing that,' said Bosh.

'Not sure that will come up as a quiz question in Bush Pointless,' said Nakano.

'Running out of conversation is not something we're going to struggle with, having these two,' said Yuki turning to Kintaro, who grunted like a stressed-out parent.

***

Yamauba, fresh from his dressing down by Mogwai, was

crossing the Kenyan border with three of Mogwai's men. He was contemplating how he was going to carry out his boss's order, which was to kidnap a full-grown elephant and bring it back to him.

I need some professional help, he thought, and reached for his cell phone as he drove. He found a number from his contacts list and pressed the call button.

Almost immediately, the call was answered.

'Yama, my friend, how the devil are you?'

'I'm well, Duplessis, you old dog … it's been a long time.'

'It sure has,' Duplessis replied, 'you only call me when you want something.'

'You're right, Dup, but I need a man with your talents,' said Yama.

'And what talents would they be?' Duplessis replied. 'I have many.'

'I know you do, you old goat. There could be a lot of rand in it for you.'

'What is the job, my friend?'

'It's capturing an elephant.'

'That is no problem. That is what I do.'

'But these are no ordinary elephants,' said Yama.

'What do you mean?' asked Duplessis, confused.

'I will tell you later, my friend. Just bring everything you need and I will meet you at the Mawe Ninja camp near to the Burungi,' said Yama.

'Okay, see you later,' Duplessis replied and hung up the phone.

That's the logistics sorted out, Yamauba thought. He continued to his next appointment, which was with Cassaire, at a location on the Mara River.

***

'Here's a question for you,' said Nakano. 'Were you afraid of any animals before you were given your powers?'

'No animals, but insects, yes. I cannot stand bees,' said Kintaro.

'Why bees? They're harmless enough,' said Nakano.

'Believe me, I have seen what a swarm of bees can do, in amongst a herd. Bees are attracted to the water around our eyes and can penetrate our thick hides. Worst of all is when they get up your trunk. We elephants go berserk,' said Kintaro.

'Really? Every day is a school day,' said Nakano.

'I don't like mice,' said Yuki. 'It's the thought of them nibbling at my feet.'

'My best friend is a mouse. An African pygmy mouse called Arthur,' said Issun, sighing. 'I miss him so much.'

'Ah – he has got a sensitive side after all,' teased Nakano.

With all this small talk going on, the group had all but reached the lake when Issun spoke up again. 'I hope there are no crocodiles in the lake.'

'Oh yes, Bosh, thanks for reminding me. I'm afraid of crocodiles too. Be aware at all times, everyone, and enter the water with care,' Kintaro said.

They approached the lake cautiously, took in some

much-needed refreshment, and Kintaro gently lowered Issun to the water's edge.

'We can wallow in this cool water while we wash, too,' said Yuki.

'Now don't use all the hot water, little one,' Kintaro joked, at which Bosh jabbed him in the trunk with his needle, making the big feller wince.

'Make the most of this rest period, everyone, and we will wait for a sign from Narok,' the big feller replied.

***

Not too far away, Yamauba was meeting with Cassaire, and her cohorts.

She was a very distinctive and sinister-looking hyena. Cassaire had something odd about her aura and she glowed as if a fire was burning within, visible from the outside.

Her only Achilles heel was her pack, which Kintaro had come across when he helped the young impala.

'So, Cassaire, are you aware of the new threat to our activities here in the bush?' asked Yamauba.

'I have heard something on the grapevine about nellies running around performing magic and making a nuisance of themselves,' she replied.

'It's not magic, Cassaire, it's fact, and you are going to help me do something about it.'

'So, what's the plan? What do you expect me to do about it?' she asked.

'Create a diversion, that's what.'

'For what purpose?' she replied. 'What do we get out of it?'

'We're going to capture one of them. I will ensure that you and your crew are rewarded handsomely,' said Yamauba. 'A friend of mine will do the capturing – that is his field of expertise.'

'That's it?' she said. 'Just create some mayhem?'

'Yes, that's it, apart from knowing their whereabouts. Any idea?' he asked.

'I might have.'

'Don't mess with me, you mangy creature,' Yama said, raising his rifle.

'Okay, big guy, calm down. I'm only having a bit of fun with you.'

'Where are they?' said Yamauba. 'My patience is running thin.'

'Patience, Yamauba. There's an old Swahili saying: "Patience attracts happiness; it brings near that which is far." They are at Lake Burungi and my warthog friend tells me that they will camp there for a few days.'

'At last, we got there in the end. You know your orders. I will meet you at the lake in two hours.'

Yamauba signalled to his men and they jumped into their vehicles to make their way to the disused camp at Mawe and rendezvous with Duplessis.

***

'You were right about the warthogs, Yuki, they stink!' said Nakano.

'It's not them, Naki, it's you who stinks,' said Bosh, paddling at the very tip of the lake.

'Shut up, Bosh, or I'll drown you with a splash.'

'Will the two of you just stop, at least for a moment, while we enjoy this spa time together?' said Kintaro.

It's great to see the local wildlife taking in what the lake has to offer, thought Yuki.

The experience lasted at least an hour before everyone dried off and thought about settling down for the evening. The winds, however, were now getting stronger and showed no signs of abating. Kintaro suggested they kept together with no late afternoon strolls on this occasion.

***

Yamauba and Duplessis had met at the Mawe Ninja camp and were already in convoy, heading towards Lake Burungi. Although the lake was not as big as the Manyara, it was big enough. The vehicles needed to navigate the circumference with great care, so as not to disturb its camping visitors.

'Take it steady,' said Yamauba to his driver.

Duplessis followed a respectful distance behind.

'We will meet Cassaire's pack any time now, so keep your eyes open for them,' Yamauba said to his men.

Cassaire was already in situ and watching proceedings from behind some shrubs. 'Do not let me down, gentlemen,' she said to her pack, 'especially you, Drach.'

He was desperately trying not to laugh and contained his affliction with a gentle snigger.

'I will give the signal when it's time. You all know what to do,' she said.

Yamauba's vehicle approached Cassaire's hiding location. He flashed his torchlight, which was the signal for the hyenas to initiate the diversion and mayhem when they were ready. His cell phone vibrated with an incoming call; it was Duplessis.

'There is a sandstorm coming, Yama. Have you seen it?'

'Yes, Dup, I've seen it. Just make sure you catch at least one of them – they will struggle to see us coming. I don't care which one, but we're not leaving without a caged elephant.' Said Yamauba.

***

The four elephants could see the curtain of sand that was about to engulf them like a tsunami.

'Huddle together, everyone,' said Yuki.

The three of them came together as one, Issun seeking protection behind one of Kintaro's huge ears.

Just as the sandstorm smothered the elephants, making it impossible to see, Cassaire signalled for her pack to play their part. The hyena's time for keeping quiet was over as they raced towards the elephants, screeching, howling, and creating mayhem.

'Hyenas!' shouted Kintaro. 'Stay together and don't move.'

'I can't see anything – what should I do?' said Nakano.

'Stay calm, Nakano, they can't hurt us if we stay together,' said Yuki.

The sandstorm was now at its peak, with absolutely no visibility and the strong winds threatening to prise the group apart. The sounds of motor vehicles and gunshots wreaked havoc. Panic set in among the other animals. Warthogs were fleeing in all directions. Impalas were colliding with each other. Zebras were making distressing calls as if they had contracted whooping cough.

The elephants' powers were useless; their formation had collapsed and they were on their own.

Men shouting, hyenas screeching, and gunfire continued, giving Duplessis and his men the opportunity to strike.

The lack of visibility meant that the elephant they chose to capture was, by chance, Kintaro, the strongest. Ropes and netting were thrown over him in an attempt to bring him to the ground.

'Quick, men, go for his legs,' said Duplessis, 'cover its head.'

As the big guy was falling, Bosh became dislodged from behind Kintaro's ear and was flung into the air, losing grip of his ivory needle at the same time.

As Issun fell towards the ground, Vossler leapt into the air and caught him mid-flight in his mouth; it was a miracle he didn't swallow him. As Vossler landed, he was knocked off his feet by Tidas, who clumsily clattered into his friend, causing Vossler to cough Issun high into the air once more. Drach saw his opportunity and, with slobbering tongue exposed, snatched Issun into his mouth, lizard style, and sped off.

At least the laughing had stopped, with Issun in his mouth, and he tried not to injure his victim. Drach, feeling quite pleased with himself, ran face on into Yamauba's four-by-four, knocking himself unconscious. This left Mortas close by to pick up the pieces and collect a dazed Issun as he scrambled out of the side of the semiconscious Drach's mouth.

Oh no, what am I going to do now? Mortas thought. *What if I swallow him? What if I bite him? What if I drop him? What will Cassaire do to me? I know, I'll pretend I never saw him and place him on the ground just here.* This he did, and ran off.

Issun was once again free, but was now on the ground, away from his needle to help him gain full height.

As the commotion continued, Narok observed from the sky and could just about make out that warthogs, people, elephants, zebras were all stampeding and narrowly missing squashing Issun, who was powerless without the ability to stamp his trusty needle onto the ground and activate his transformation.

Issun looked up to the sky and through the storm saw Narok as the curtain of sand started to clear, giving him some visibility at least.

He turned around and, to his horror, came face to face with a pouched rat. *This is it*, he thought, *I've had it.* The rat was immediately squashed by Zul, who at the same time scooped up Bosh in his mouth and carried him to safety, away from the melee.

Cassaire, for her part, watched her bumbling cohorts making a warthog's ear out of what should have been a simple task, but had the presence of mind to spot Issun's needle glistening in the dust. She remembered the story of Bosh defending the baboons against Rhazien, her arch-enemy, and that Issun used the needle to initiate his power. It was like actually finding a needle in a haystack; she picked it up and carried it with her. *It will make a good toothpick, if nothing else*, she thought.

***

'We're wasting our time, men – this elephant is too strong,' said Duplessis and he ordered his men to retreat.

'Leave it for now,' said Yamauba. 'Return to the Mawe camp. We can try again later.'

Kintaro was left by his assailants and freed himself from the weighted nets partially covering him.

Narok had seen exactly what had happened. He swooped down to where the three remaining elephants had just found each other, none of them realising that Issun had been taken. 'Is everyone okay?' he asked.

'Yes, we think so,' said Yuki. 'What just happened?'

'There was an attempt to kidnap one of you.'

'Thank the gods they failed,' said Nakano.

'I'm sorry, Nakano,' said Narok, 'but they succeeded.'

'But we're all here and Issun is behind my …' said Kintaro, hesitating and searching for Issun behind his ear with his trunk. 'He's not there!'

'I'm afraid they got to him and he's gone,' said Narok.

'Do you think he's still alive?' Nakano asked.

'He is alive, but he will need our help.'

'We have to rescue him,' said Yuki. 'Do you know where they have taken him?'

'Yes. We will rescue him, but you will have to trust me to find a way. Please stay here and I will let you know what to do next,' Narok said.

'Thank you, we will await your further instructions, but please hurry,' said Kintaro.

***

An hour or so later, Yamauba and Duplessis arrived back at the disused safari camp at Mawe, Cassaire not far behind them.

'Well, that was a complete disaster!' said Yamauba. 'What went wrong, Dup? You said you were the expert and could handle this?'

'It's hard enough catching animals, but impossible in a sandstorm,' Dup replied.

Seconds later, Cassaire and her bedraggled pack entered the room where Yamauba and Duplessis were still contesting who was to blame.

'Mogwai will kill me!' said Yama.

'Before he does,' said Cassaire coolly, 'we did our bit and we want paying for our services.'

'Paying!' said Yama. 'We failed. How can you expect to be paid?'

'Fail,' said Cassaire, 'means First Attempt In Learning.'

'Oh, shut up, Cassaire, with your smart words. You're getting nothing,' Yama replied.

The three-way argument was interrupted by the sound of Zul making a vomiting-dog sound and shaping his body as if to throw up.

Splat! Out came Bosh, covered in hyena slobber.

'Sorry guys, I forgot I had him in my mouth,' he said apologetically.

'What the hell is that?' asked Yama and Dup in unison.

'There is your elephant,' said Cassaire, taking all the glory.

'But it's … it's tiny. How could it possibly be of value to Mogwai?' said Yamauba.

'As he is now,' said Cassaire, 'no value at all, but with this,' she produced Issun's ivory needle, 'he's worth a fortune.'

'What do you mean? Explain yourself, Cassaire,' said Yama.

'Put this needle with him and you have an elephant with the power to become fully grown. Skilled at using it too,' she said. 'Make sure you keep them apart. Now, can we get paid please?'

'All in good time, Cassaire,' said Yamauba. He picked up the shaken Issun and carefully placed him in an old mesh frying basket with a lid. The gaps were too small for Issun to escape. He locked it with a small padlock and placed the key in his utility belt pocket and the needle in a separate one. 'Mission complete.'

13

The Rescue

Arthur's theme

Narok flew through the night to get to the baobab residence of Swiss and Perrin, arriving at dawn and intending to try and persuade Arthur to help his friend escape the clutches of Yamauba.

He knew they had little time to secure Bosh's freedom. Mogwai already had a buyer lined up for a captured elephant and the idea of one of them living in a circus or freak show did not bear thinking about.

Swiss and Perrin had already risen and looked to the sky to see Narok coming into land.

'I hope everything is okay,' Swiss said to Perrin, seeing Narok make his approach.

'Do you think it's about Issun?' Perrin replied.

'Maybe Bosh is with him?' Swiss said. Both instinctively knew that as the visit was unscheduled it was unlikely to be a social call.

The martial eagle landed to the side of their homestead and hopped his way towards the oncoming foster parents.

'Good day to you both,' he said, 'and my apologies for such an early intrusion to your day.'

'What is it, Narok? Is everything okay? Is Issun okay?' Swiss asked.

'I have some news about Issun Boshi but don't worry, he is fine,' Narok replied.

'Please tell us, Narok, what has happened to him,' Perrin said.

'Bosh has been kidnapped by poachers led by their cowardly leader called Yamauba.'

'Kidnapped? Where, how, why?' Perrin asked, fighting back tears of concern.

'Issun and his friends were ambushed in a sandstorm at the Burungi Lake by poachers and hyenas. They stood little chance,' said Narok.

'What about the others? Could they not help little Issun?' asked Swiss.

'It was impossible to see anything because of the storm, but their assailants were well organised and the hyenas were the ones to snatch poor Issun away,' Narok replied.

'Where have they taken him?' the two baboons asked simultaneously.

'I followed from a distance and they took him to a disused safari camp, not far from the Burungi, called Mawe Ninja, but I fear Yamauba will be keen to get Issun away from there as quickly as possible,' said Narok. 'Hence the need for my visit. I need some help to try and rescue him.'

'We will do anything … anything, Narok, to help save Issun,' said Swiss.

'Yes, tell us how we can help,' said Perrin.

'I know the two of you would lay down your lives for Issun, but you can help in a very subtle way,' Narok replied.

'Just tell us,' said Swiss impatiently.

'Do you still have Arthur with you?' Narok asked.

'Yes, we do. Why do you ask?' said Perrin.

'I ask because Issun was taken in his normal size and separated from his needle, rendering him unable to use his powers. I will need Arthur's size and abilities to penetrate the camp and help free him,' Narok said.

'Quick, go and wake him, Perrin,' said Swiss.

Perrin raced inside their home, emerging shortly after with a bleary-eyed Arthur.

'What's wrong?' asked Arthur. 'Is it Issun? Is he okay?'

'He needs your help, Arthur. Are you willing to help him?' said Swiss.

'Do fish swim?' replied Arthur. 'Of course, I would do anything for Bosh.'

'Thank you, Arthur,' said Narok. 'Please climb aboard and I will explain everything on the way.'

Arthur leapt onto Narok's wing and the two said their farewells and took flight.

***

'Good morning, squirt. How is everything in tiny elephant land this morning?' said Yamauba.

'You won't keep me here for long, Yama Daba Doo, or whatever it is they call you,' Bosh replied.

'So, you think your friends are coming to save you?'

'I do,' Issun replied. 'None of the Tamonten Tusks are ever left behind.'

'How will they know where you are? Or whether you are still alive?' Yama asked.

'I have friends in high places. Friends you could only dream about,' Bosh replied.

'Oh, I see, you mean the gods of the savanna? They will save you?'

'Good will always prevail over evil, you'll see,' said Bosh.

'Well, the gods will have to be quick – we're leaving for the city in an hour.' Yamauba turned to the men Mogwai had given him to assist with the kidnapping and ordered them to pack their equipment and ready the truck for the journey to Mombasa.

***

'I'm worried sick about Issun,' said Yuki.

'We'll get him back, try not to worry,' said Kintaro.

'I'm even starting to miss his annoying quips,' said Nakano.

'Is there nothing we can do for him?'

'We have to trust in Narok, ladies. He will know exactly where Bosh is, and how to rescue him. I am also sure he will let us know what part we play in getting Bosh back.'

Yuki believed that what Kintaro was saying made sense, but she could not stay and do nothing. She quietly slipped away from the lake without the others knowing.

Yuki believed that if she followed the poachers' tracks, she could find their hideout and get some intel for when Narok arrived.

***

Back at the Mawe Ninja camp, Yamauba was talking to his boss on his cell phone.

'Yes, Mogwai, we have one of them for you and you will not be disappointed,' said Yamauba.

'Good work. Which one do you have for me?' asked Mogwai.

'I have the one who will give you the least amount of trouble – the so-called inch-high samurai. He is the easiest to transport. He's tiny, and I have him locked up in a miniature cage,' said Yamauba.

'Excellent,' replied Mogwai, 'bring it to me immediately.'

'We're almost ready, boss, just tying up a few loose ends here and we'll be on our way.' Yamauba hung up and ordered one of his men to prepare the outside shower. He did not want to present the prize to Mogwai smelling of warthog.

***

Yuki had managed to trace the tyre tracks all the way to the lodge. Outside, in her invisible state, she listened to the whole conversation Yama had with both his boss and

126

his men. She backed away slowly and gradually returned to visibility again, taking cover among some nearby trees.

I hope my power will return soon, she thought, *I'm going to need it.*

Moments later she caught a glimpse of Narok landing just a few metres away.

She beckoned. 'Psst, Narok, it's me, Yuki, over here.'

Narok hopped towards her. 'What are you doing here?' he whispered. 'I said I would advise you as to what to do next.'

'I know you did, Narok. I'm sorry for sneaking away. I felt I had to do something.'

'I have a plan already, Yuki, and it involves one of Issun's closest friends.'

The little mouse emerged from beneath Narok's feathers. 'Hello, Yuki. My name is Arthur.'

'Nice to meet you, Arthur, although I wish it was in better circumstances. How are we going to get Issun out of this mess?'

'I have brought Arthur here to help because of his size and capabilities. Just how we can use his abilities I have yet to figure out,' said Narok.

'Maybe I can help?' said Yuki. 'I have managed to listen to several conversations while I was outside the lodge, and I know what Yamauba's plans are. But we don't have much time. What I do know is that Issun is locked in a small cage, and I know where the key is. Yama also has his ivory needle.'

'Where is it?' Arthur asked.

'They are both in his utility belt. He plans to take a shower before they leave for the port of Mombasa,' she replied.

'That's our opportunity. He must remove it to take a shower,' Narok said.

'If I can get Arthur to the belt while Yama is taking his shower, we have half a chance,' said Yuki.

'Let's do it,' Arthur said. 'But how can you get me to it without being seen?'

'It's a long story, Arthur, but Narok gave me a power too. I just hope it returns for long enough.'

'You have to concentrate, Yuki, and focus,' said Narok.

She closed her eyes and concentrated, fuelled by the will to help set Issun free. A few seconds later the change in Yuki started, her lower half the first to disappear.

'Wow!' said Arthur.

Soon after, the rest of her body completely disappeared.

Yuki picked Arthur up with her trunk and they quietly made their way to the outhouse window where Yamauba was taking his shower. The shower was rather primitive. It consisted of a bucket, raised or lowered by a wire cable, a stopcock, and a rusty metal shower rose. The idea was that the user controlled how much water came out via the stopcock wheel – not quite a thermostatically controlled power shower with body jets.

Through an open window they could see Yamauba's belt, hanging on a hook next to the shower cubicle.

Yuki gently lowered Arthur inside with her trunk and onto the hook, from where he lowered himself onto the belt and entered one of the pockets.

To Arthur's surprise, the first pocket he investigated contained the small padlock key. However, it was not small to someone of Arthur's size. Fortunately, it was not too heavy and Arthur clung on to it for dear life. 'At least I have the key,' he said to himself. 'Just need to find Bosh's needle.'

Yuki and Arthur's timing was to perfection. No sooner had Arthur hidden inside the belt pocket than Yamauba finished taking his shower and began towelling down before getting dressed. He started with his trousers, then unhooked the utility belt and fastened it around his waist. Next, he put on a T-shirt, followed by a chest rig holster with a diagonal leather strap across his back. Sitting inside the belt pocket, Arthur could sense movement, back and forth, up and down, as Yamauba put on his socks and boots.

Fully dressed, Yamauba made his way back inside the lodge and sat down at the table, where Issun was imprisoned in the small mesh cage.

'Now then, Bish Bash Bosh, or whatever it is they call you. We're leaving soon and I want to explain our next steps. We have a fairly long trip ahead of us.'

This was Arthur's opportunity to make his move.

He gingerly climbed out of the first pocket with the key and made his way to another open pocket on the other side of the clasp, towards Yama's left hip.

Bingo! He had chosen the pocket containing Issun's needle. *I am one lucky mouse.*

He started to climb up the strap of Yama's chest holster, carefully ensuring that he did not touch any other part of Yamauba's back. This was no mean feat; the key was heavy enough, but the needle was the size of a kendo pole to Arthur.

He carefully threaded the needle through the hole at the top of the key, put it over his shoulder and climbed higher, taking advantage of Yama's distraction while he talked to Issun. Once he reached Yama's left shoulder, he saw his friend down below on the table. Taking some cover from Yama's upturned collar, he waved at Bosh.

In complete disbelief, Issun recognised his friend immediately. It took most of his self-control not to let out a scream of excitement. Maintaining his composure, Issun pretended to listen to Yamauba, stalling for time by asking further questions.

What am I going to do now? Arthur thought, perched high on the tall man's shoulder.

Meanwhile, Yuki was watching from the window of the lodge, still invisible. *I have to do something,* she thought, *I need to create some sort of diversion.* The first thing that came into her head was to kick the door down, which was exactly what she did.

Yama, startled, turned around to see who was there. This gave Arthur his opportunity to leap off Yama's shoulder and onto the table to free his friend.

Yamauba ran to the door, completely oblivious to

Arthur's presence. Accompanied by his men, they saw Yuki, semi-visible, running from the lodge.

'Get her!' Yama shouted, and his men gave chase into the bush.

Yama turned around to be confronted by Issun Boshi, fully grown, standing in a defiant pose and brandishing his ivory needle outstretched to his right.

'Oh heck!' he said and ran outside where his men had returned, empty-handed. 'Don't just stand there, get the elephant inside the lodge.'

The three deputies ran inside, not realising that Issun had morphed to full size. 'Hello, gentlemen,' he said.

Bosh sprang into a display of weapons prowess, skilfully manoeuvring his ivory needle from side to side, up and down, inside and out, like a nun-chuck expert. This display of martial arts skills was enough to persuade the men to flee in all directions rather than face the mighty Issun Boshi in full flow.

By now, the cowardly Yamauba was already in one of the pickup trucks, racing away from the scene, stirring up clouds of dust from all four wheels.

'You did it, Bosh, you escaped,' said Arthur.

'Thanks to you, Arthur – you rescued me and I cannot thank you enough.'

'Oh, stop it, Bosh, you would have done the same for me.'

Yuki and Narok joined them from the bush and heaped praise on Arthur's bravery.

They were soon joined by the three remaining Tusks,

who had set out in search of Yuki.

'Swiss and Perrin will never believe me,' said Arthur.

'Oh, but they will, my friend. Say your farewells for now and hop aboard. We need to get you back to your family,' said Narok.

They took off; Arthur waved, feeling pretty pleased with himself.

14

Veruca

An unfortunate name

Veruca Wu was obsessed with ivory artefacts. Someone had once told her that ivory symbolised status and wealth in Chinese culture. This was something she could afford now, given the success of her TV chat show, *V*.

She was considered the Oprah Winfrey of Hong Kong.

The show aired every Monday and Wednesday on TVB Hong Kong at 9 p.m., and she was grateful to have had a say in the show's title. Not that she hated her first name, but it was synonymous with a type of wart on the foot and was not particularly flattering.

Veruca's mother had had an obsession with anything Roald Dhal, so her name was taken from a character in *Charlie and the Chocolate Factory*.

Her show had been running for two years and station executives had agreed to a five-year extension to her contract, should she stay with TVB. At thirty, this was her dream come true, and afforded her most of life's luxuries in Honk Kong, including a very stylish pad in West Kowloon.

She was an extremely attractive lady, with soft wavy jet-black hair, and a strong resemblance to Lucy Liu from another Charlie TV show, *Charlie's Angels*.

Aside from her obvious good looks, she was also intelligent, witty, charming, and tactful, if not a little naïve at times. Her friends often teased her when she came out with something 'not quite right'.

In terms of her obsession with ivory, she was always on the lookout for something different to add to her collection, constantly challenging the proprietor of the Chinese art shop based in the Admiralty District of Hong Kong Island. She visited the shop regularly, between recordings, often just chatting with the owner, Li Quiang, without making a purchase. He knew her taste well and would call her when something special came in.

During one of their chats in his shop, Li suggested that Veruca might enjoy a safari holiday in Africa for her next vacation. She thought that was an excellent idea and promptly booked time off with the station executives for the end of the current series, which had only two episodes left to record.

The safari was booked by her agent with one of Kenya's best safari holiday companies, 'Deepest Africa', to begin in ten days.

***

I'm so looking forward to this experience, she thought upon arrival at Jomo Kenyatta International Airport, Nairobi.

Veruca was met by the safari company's representative, who was holding a tablet with her name on it and had a chauffeur-driven limousine waiting outside.

She was driven to the exclusive Cottars 1920s safari hotel.

This was located in the south-east corner of the Maasai Mara, near the Tanzanian border and would be her home for the next ten days.

V instantly fell in love with Africa. The sights and sounds were to die for, even before she had encountered a single animal.

Her first full day was spent relaxing in the resort, enjoying the spa facilities and swimming pool. Staff in the resort could not have been more accommodating.

V found it amusing that they already had a nickname for her, which was G22, the room number she used to sign for drinks and so on.

The following day she awoke early, having not had much sleep, and got dressed in her brand new safari attire, recommended by a close friend from her chat show's wardrobe department.

The day could not have started any better, she thought. The weather was fantastic and her fellow safari-goers seemed pleasant enough.

***

The group had not been travelling for very long when the guides stopped the vehicle to allow their clients to see a group of giraffes feeding on acacia trees conveniently at head height.

That was beautiful to see, she thought, snapping away to capture the memory.

'I mustn't do too much of that,' she said aloud; Li had told her not to take too many pictures, just to photograph the splendour with her eyes. *Great advice*, she thought, but could not help herself and carried on taking photos.

The tour guides were knowledgeable and kept their paying clients spellbound with more amazing experiences until they encountered a scene with some vulture activity.

'Drive on,' said the tour leader, but one of the men aboard spoke out and asked to investigate further. 'I have paid to experience the real Africa and would like to appreciate nature in its purest form,' said the client.

This alarmed V; she didn't know what was happening or what the man meant when he said 'its purest form'.

The guide turned to V and said, 'I would not recommend that you see this, madam. It will not be very nice.'

'What do you mean?' V replied.

'An animal has been killed. I suggest you stay here a while and we will resume in a few minutes.'

Something came over V and her journalistic mind got the better of her. 'I want to see what's out there.' She climbed out of the truck, following the outspoken gentleman, and headed to where the vultures were. The vultures took off at the sight of the tourists.

'Oh my god,' said the man, 'this is not an animal killed for food. It has to be poachers.'

'Why?' said V, trying to get closer. To her horror, she saw that the stricken animal was a full-grown elephant with its tusks hacked out. The sight and stench were overwhelming for V and she turned away in shock.

'Why has someone done this?' she asked the man.

'Ivory, for so-called art,' he replied.

V was mortified and was overcome with tears. The man put his arm around her shoulder to comfort her and escorted her back to the truck. Veruca was utterly ashamed. She hardly paid any attention to the rest of the tour and wished it would end soon.

It was no surprise to Veruca that she did not get any sleep that night; she just couldn't get the gruesome image of the dead elephant out of her head. She felt myriad emotions – sorrow, anguish, grief, and naivety.

Where did I think ivory came from? she thought. *Did I think it grew on trees?* 'No,' she said out loud, 'you are an idiot, Veruca!'

The next day, she declined the scheduled tour and pottered around the hotel, thinking about her life so far, and what was important in terms of where to go from here.

Day five was to be another trek into the bush.

V had come to terms with what she had witnessed on day three and had arrived at the conclusion that she should use the opportunity to educate herself about the reality of life in Africa.

The morning was spent in the bush and the afternoon was a scheduled visit to a Maasai Mara village, which she was looking forward to.

Upon arrival at the village, the group could not have received a friendlier welcome from the villagers, who offered the guests the option of drinking cow's blood or milk, a Maasai tradition. V opted for the latter, so as not to offend the locals, who giggled at her choice.

The group were shown around the houses, called kraals. These were arranged in a circle, loaf-shaped, and made out of mud, dung, and sticks, grass, and cow's urine.

The party was divided into six groups of two guests each, and V was paired with a Filipino lady called Thelma. Their Maasai guide was called Johari, which in Swahili meant 'something precious', 'to be adored' or 'jewel'.

Johari took the two women to one of the kraals, where they found several other women making what looked like beautiful jewellery. Each one of them was modelling the various necklaces, headbands, bracelets, and earrings they were making.

'What amazing colours ... do they represent anything?' V asked Johari.

'Yes, they do. First of all, women consider it their duty to craft jewellery to be worn by both men and women. The colour and structure of the necklaces indicate someone's age, marital status, and can even show if a woman has given birth to a boy or a girl,' said Johari.

'What do the colours mean?' asked V.

'Each of the colours represents something relating to

cattle, because cattle are our main food source,' Johari replied.

'Fascinating,' said Thelma.

'Red symbolises bravery and strength, the colour of cow's blood. Blue represents the sky, which creates rain for the cattle. Green stands for land, which grows food for the cattle. Orange and yellow represent hospitality, because they are the colour of cattle skins we place on guests' beds. Lastly, black symbolises the people and the struggles they endure.'

'They are beautiful,' said V, 'can I buy some?'

'Of course,' Johari replied, and both ladies chose several fine examples of genuine home-made Maasai Mara jewellery from this unique cottage industry.

Veruca was fascinated by Johari and Maasai tradition and wanted to learn more about her tribe. Her questions were welcomed by the Maasai lady and answered with pride.

One of the things Veruca was keen to learn more about was the tribe's interaction with wildlife in the savanna – which animals were they most afraid of and how did they protect themselves against dangerous predators? She also had a question about the famous warriors; she understood that a young Maasai man could not be considered a warrior until he had hunted solo and killed a lion. 'Is this true?' she asked.

'This is a myth,' Johari replied. 'Many people believe that young men single-handedly kill lions to impress the girls or that it's a rite of passage to signify that a young man has become a skilful warrior. However, the truth is that men skilled in hunting do occasionally attack lions with their spears if they felt their cattle are being threatened. Since the decline in lion populations the men only hunt lions in groups, but never for food, and they would never hunt a female because they are seen as the bearers of life.'

'What other animals do you fear?' Veruca asked.

'The elephant is a cause for concern for us, although we do not dislike them and they remind us of our own family values, but they often stray into our villages, causing damage to property and help themselves to our crops. In fact, I have a story which will amaze you and will be remembered in Maasai folklore for centuries.'

'Please tell us, Johari,' V asked impatiently.

'A short time ago, when everyone was sleeping, our village came under attack from stampeding elephants we believe were spooked by poachers and were headed in the direction of our houses.'

'Please go on, Johari.'

'Many of the women, including myself, were alerted by the chief as to the threat and we tended to the children, but it was difficult to know how best to protect them. As the devastation was about to unfold, the chief spotted a huge white elephant at the entrance to our village and facing the oncoming charging herd.'

'What did it do?'

'The great white elephant was no doubt sent by our god Ingai Narok to protect us, and the chief ordered everyone in the village to hide behind its massive frame. One by one, the elephants were brushed away from trampling us to death, but still they kept coming. It is our belief that the great white elephant was bestowed with incredible strength and the stamina to save our people. We only suffered the loss of some homes and crops.'

'That really is an amazing story, Johari, and one I will never forget. Thank you for sharing that with us.'

***

The adventure in Africa had been a life-changing experience for Veruca. One of the first things she did when she got home was to collect all the ivory artefacts she had. Every bearded man holding a scroll, every temple, and every collection of wise monkeys, and burned them in her garden, paying no attention to their value whatsoever.

This was something she felt that she had to do and was liberating for her. She vowed to use her TV platform to raise awareness about the senseless killing of elephants and rhinos for so-called art, status, and pleasure.

Veruca presented a plan to the producers of her chat show to highlight that the ivory trade in Hong Kong and the rest of the world would be illegal by the end of 2021.

Social media would also be used to promote how uncool it was to display such grotesque pieces in households throughout the world.

She also contacted some entrepreneurial friends of hers to look into the importation of genuine Maasai Mara jewellery and promote as an ongoing fashion trend.

Veruca felt that the experience had enriched her outlook on life and that there were many untold stories of heroism like that of the great white elephant, which she felt needed sharing.

15

Bees

Honey, I shrunk the Bosh

Monar loved working on his farm, continuing the family tradition. They had managed it for generations. Although it was small at barely a hectare, he was able to grow crops to help feed his family.

Unfortunately the climate, with long periods of drought, often threatened his farm's survival, a greater threat came from nomadic elephants who frequently trampled and fed on his crops. He had considered shooting them but could not bring himself to killing one of the most majestic animals in Africa. Monar believed that they had more right to be there than him, given that they had descended from mammoths so many years ago.

At fifty-eight years of age, Monar, whose name was slave-related, looked older than his years. His weathered face sported a goatee beard and a distinct lack of teeth. He wore shabby long trousers with an unbuttoned shirt, untidily left outside rather than being tucked in. He did own a suit, though, which he kept in a cardboard box in his wardrobe. He had vowed only to wear it at his daughter's wedding.

It was the weekend and Monar was picking sweet potatoes in his field when he saw vehicles approaching. There were three – a Land Rover, a people carrier, and a medium-sized lorry.

Who can this be? he thought. *Better not be government people coming to take my land or charge me rent.*

The convoy of vehicles whipped up a cloud of dust on the makeshift drive up to his house and came to a stop. A very distinguished-looking white gentleman stepped out and greeted him, arm outstretched as if to shake hands.

'Hello, Monar, my name is Max. Please don't be alarmed – my apologies for the impromptu visit.'

'How can I help you, Mr Max, are you lost?' said Monar shaking the man's hand.

'No, not at all,' Dr Max replied, 'I have been told all about you and others like you, trying to make a living continuing the tradition of farming that must have been in your families for generations.'

'Well, that's very nice of you to say, Mr Max, but why have you come to my house today?' Monar asked.

'The reason for my visit is to try and help you with an issue I know you must find frustrating, namely the impact elephants have on your lives here.'

'Yes, it is, but what can I do?' Monar replied. 'Other than pray to the gods that they leave me alone.'

'I totally understand, Monar. I too respect elephants

and I am deeply concerned for their well-being. However, I have a potential solution that could help both the elephants and yourself.'

'What solution would that be?'

'It is an experimental idea, with no cost to you. We would like to erect a type of fence around your property to keep the elephants away from your crops,' said Max.

'I don't want a fence, Mr Max. There has not been a fence here in my family's history, and we don't want to block out the view of the lands we live among.'

'Please, let me explain. The fence I refer to will not restrict your views – it is a fence made out of bees,' Dr Max replied.

'Bees! Are you joking with me, Mr Max?' said Monar.

'No, sir, I am completely serious. I'm not sure if you are aware, but elephants are afraid of bees. They will run away rather than get stung or suffer the discomfort of bees in their trunks.'

'I had no idea,' said Monar, 'but I still don't understand how you intend to use them.'

'It's quite simple, really, and I can't take credit for the idea. We have constructed beehives from carbon fibre and will hang them from the trees surrounding your property. The hives will be connected to each other with wire, and when they are disturbed by elephants, the hives rock back and forth. This causes the bees to be alarmed. They will then swarm and become very vocal. Elephants are afraid of the noise, realise the threat, and leave immediately,' said Dr Max.

'That sounds like it could work, but I'm on my own here. I have no one to help me construct such a fence,' Monar replied.

'Don't worry about that. I have a team with me today, complete with hives, bees, and everything we need to finish the project. All I ask is that you give us some feedback as to its effectiveness,' said Dr Max.

'Thank you. Of course I will monitor the experiment. We will call it the David and Goliath Project,' Monar replied.

'One other thing I should mention is that the bees will produce honey on a large scale for you and your family to enjoy. Plus the potential to bottle and sell it in the markets.'

'That could make a huge difference to my family's future, Mr Max. The gods must have listened to my prayers after all.'

'Let's start straight away – it should only take a day or so to erect. I will ask my team to commence construction. All we ask is that you allow us to camp overnight on your land and an occasional cup of tea. Is that okay with you?'

'That's the least we can do. My wife will make you and your men some food too,' Monar replied.

Dr Max ordered his men to unload the materials and helped them get to work, erecting a living fence around Monar's farm.

***

The following day, the Tamonten Tusks were making their way north, waiting for some much-needed direction from Narok.

'I know we are a nomadic species,' said Bosh, 'but should that term be changed to *no-mad-idea where we're going?*'

'Very funny,' Kintaro replied. 'If we were going in the wrong direction, Narok would show us.'

'I hope so. We have been wandering now for about four days and nothing exciting has happened. I'm getting quite bored,' said Bosh.

'Don't speak too soon, Bosh. We have been very fortunate so far, and no harm has come to any of us,' said Yuki.

'Bosh is right, Yuki, although it pains me to admit it,' said Nakano. 'None of us has any idea what our destiny is.'

'We must trust in Narok and be patient. It will all make sense soon enough,' said Kintaro.

The four elephants were heading in a northerly direction towards the Arusha National Park, quite close to the Kenyan border.

'I'm hungry,' said Bosh.

'Hungry? I could pick up a leaf and it would keep you going for a month,' Nakano said.

'We should stop for food though,' Yuki suggested.

The four decided that taking a break for food and rest was a good idea. A few minutes later, they spotted a suitable location.

'This looks like a good place to stop. We can eat and relax a while,' said Issun as they approached a sheltered area with plenty of trees and sweet potatoes in the ground.

'Perfect,' said Nakano.

The spot they had chosen was on the far side of Monar's farm.

Kintaro and Bosh were first to meander through some of the plentiful trees, looking for food. The girls followed, taking a similar path between two trees.

Seconds after walking amongst the trees, Kintaro felt a cold metallic wire press against his chest. 'What the heck was that?' he said.

Issun added, 'What are those boxes swinging from the trees? Is it a trap? Have we walked into a trap?'

The penny dropped as the group heard a sound like the roar of an ocean.

It was bees.

'Bees!' shouted Kintaro in a fit of panic. The haunting continuous hum resonated from an identical box in front of the girls.

Instantly, thousands of bees were swarming in amongst them, their wings beating like drones and flying around as fast as a warthog in a hurry.

Sheer panic set in. Kintaro was completely terror-stricken and jumped, kicked, and flapped his ears like he had stepped on a porcupine. Instinctively, he uprooted a tree and started waving it about in an attempt to use its branches and leaves to keep the bees away from him, Bosh desperately trying to cling on to his head.

Bosh came face to face with swaying tentacles and two of the biggest eyes he had ever seen. It was a stand-off; Bosh was confronted by an angry buzzing bee about a third of his size.

'Do you feel lucky, punk?' said Toni, the bee.

Although Kintaro was in a state of frenzy beneath him, Bosh slammed his needle into Kintaro's head, adding pain to his friend's mounting problems. Instantly, Bosh morphed into full size with his legs wrapped around the big K's ears.

The weight was too much for Kintaro, and the two elephants collapsed to the ground like sacks of potatoes, ironically next to a patch of sweet potatoes, growing in neatly cultivated rows.

The bees were now enjoying themselves and exchanging conversations with each other in what appeared to be an Italian accent.

'What's the matter with these a crazy elephants, Fabio?' Angelo asked.

'Don't a ask a me hey, they seem to be doing La Macarena,' Fabio replied.

'You got no respect, hey, don't a walk away from me, big ears,' said Angelo to the retreating Nakano.

Yuki, on the other hand, thought it was a good idea to disappear, which she did, but no one told the bees that she had vanished. They attached themselves to her outline, making her clearly visible to Nakano, who wielded her kendo pole, striking Yuki several times in an attempt to remove the bees from her friend's body.

'So you want to play rough, hey? Okay, say ciao to my little friend, Enzo,' said Frankie, as he and Enzo made their way to torment Nakano.

The two bees flew up inside her trunk and she vividly remembered Kintaro's recollection of a 'bee up your trunk'!

'Get out,' she cried, then sneezed, ejecting Enzo and Frankie and attracting more and more bees to join in the fun.

'Why you look so mad, tough lady?' said Enzo. 'We are just bees, no!'

Frankie hovered in mid-air in front of Nakano and warned, 'Now, Bella, if I ever, I mean ever see you here again, you die, just like that.'

The commotion was interrupted by several men in white protective clothing, wearing masks. Each of them had a metal can, which emitted smoke in the bees' direction.

'This a smoke is a making me sleepy,' said Fabio. 'Let's take a de nap, everybody.'

The bees soon calmed down and ceased their attack on the elephant intruders, returning to their hives, mission accomplished.

'Is everyone okay?' said a voice from behind a mask.

'Get off me, Bosh!' said Kintaro as Issun's body reduced in size, allowing his friend to get to his feet.

The man who had asked the question removed his mask.

'Dr Max, is that you?' said Nakano, recognising the

doctor who had rescued her and Boots.

'It is me, Nakano. How are you? Apart from a little sore with bee stings.'

'It's so good to see you again. You're right, I am a little sore and my trunk feels completely numb. I guess I'm okay though.'

The others got to their feet and realised that this must have been the kind gentleman who had rescued Nakano from her time in Thailand.

'We're very pleased to meet you, Dr Max. Thank you for helping us out of this hopeless situation with the bees. We elephants have no idea how to deal with them,' said Yuki.

Monar, who was standing next to Dr Max, removed his mask and turned to his new friend. 'Well, I guess this is your first bit of feedback, Mr Max – your beehive fence really works.'

'Indeed it does, but I see we have a tree to replant tomorrow,' said the doctor.

'Yes, sorry about that,' said Kintaro.

The doctor and Monar explained the concept behind the bee fence to the elephants, who understood, despite its severity.

'What are you doing here, Dr Max?' Nakano asked.

'Apart from project work like this one with Monar, I'm here for the summit at the United Nations headquarters in Nairobi in five days,' he replied.

'May I ask what the summit is about?' said Yuki.

'It's about numerous issues, Yuki, but I will be there

to speak about conservation and, in particular, the threat to endangered species.'

The elephants came to the conclusion that maybe the summit had something to do with their destiny.

Yuki was the first to speak up and state the obvious. 'Perhaps this summit is related to Narok's plans for us?'

'I have heard about Narok, but I understood from our friends the Maasai people that Ngai Narok was one of their gods,' the doctor replied.

'Oh, he's a god, alright,' said Issun, 'but he let us walk into this hornets' nest!'

'They're bees,' said Monar.

'Why don't you join us back at the farmhouse and you can tell me all about your adventures so far,' said Dr Max.

They all agreed and enjoyed tea and honey, with much to catch up on.

16

A Cunning Plan

Summit's about to go pear-shaped!

'Change of plan, Yarpie,' Mogwai said on the cell phone to Yamauba.

'What have I said about you calling me that,' Yama replied.

'Yeah, yeah!' Mogwai replied. 'Anyway, there's a change of plan, like I said. I now want to see you in Arusha – and where's my elephant?'

'Well, I did have one,' said Yama.

'But you messed that one up too,' Mogwai replied. 'Anyway, it does not matter. I have something more important for someone of your limited skills.'

'If you keep disrespecting me, Moggi, I will kill you,' Yama said.

'I'm only teasing, Yamauba, don't be so sensitive,' said Mogwai. 'Do you know the Peace recreation park in Arusha?'

'Yes, I have heard of it,' Yama replied.

'There's an outdoor picnic area, near to the kiddies' playground. Meet us there in an hour,' said Mogwai.

'Shall I bring some burgers, sausages, and soda?' said Yama.

'Just be there, Yarpie,' said Mogwai, abruptly ending the call.

Yamauba continued driving but altered his destination from Mombasa to Arusha, in the north of Tanzania. He was completely unaware that Narok was following closely behind.

Almost an hour after the call, Yamauba's four-by-four pulled up in the car park of the Peace recreation ground.

What's the little Chinese twerp got in store for me now? he thought. *And when he referred to* us, *who did he mean?*

This question was soon answered when he approached the picnic area and spotted Mogwai and 'friends' sitting at a family-sized table in the shade of some tall trees.

The trees were the perfect cover for Narok, who was on a surveillance mission to find out what the rascals were up to.

'You're late,' said Mogwai, trying to put Yama on the back foot.

'So what?' Yama replied. 'Who are these clowns?'

Yama indicated Cassaire, Maake, Duplessis, and Rhazien, who was continually snarling at Cassaire, his rival in the wild.

'Who are you calling a clown?' said Maake.

Yama reached for his pistol.

'Calm down, everyone, let's all be friends – and that means you hyenas too,' said Mogwai. 'I have brought you here today to help me with a plan that, if successful, will see you wealthy beyond your dreams. You will become partners in my ever-expanding empire, here in this great continent of Africa.'

'What plan is that?' asked Duplessis.

'In a few days, there will be a summit meeting involving government officials and dignitaries from all over the world, representing conservationists, landowners, farmers, villagers, and tourism companies, all meeting at the United Nations headquarters in Nairobi. They will be discussing laws relating to endangered species and putting at risk the thirty thousand elephant tusks and rhino horns I export every year,' said Mogwai.

'I guess that will cut your profits dramatically,' said Rhazien.

'Making us hunt for our food, instead of feeding off dead elephant corpses,' said Cassaire.

'Exactly the case,' said Mogwai.

'But how does that benefit me? I have no problems feeding myself,' said Maake.

'I understand. We already know that you are the King of the Savannas. I will make you my right-hand man, promote you to my bodyguard, and allow you to be king of the cities too,' Mogwai said convincingly.

'So how do you think you are going to influence legislation?' asked Yama.

'I cannot, via the democratic route,' he explained. 'This is where you all come in. An assassination!' Mogwai revealed.

'Assassinating who, all of them?' said Maake.

'No, not all of them – some will agree with ivory trade anyway. Just one delegate,' Mogwai said.

'Who is so important for you to single out as such a threat, Mogwai?' Yama asked.

'Dr Maximilian Schwarz.'

'Who the heck is Maximilian Schwarz?' asked Rhazien.

'He's a billionaire, conservationist, irritant, dedicating his life to protecting endangered animals and in particular elephants. If we take him out in front of everyone at the summit, the rest will be afraid to vote for his beliefs in fear of their own lives.'

'What roles do you want us to play in this plan, Mogwai?' asked Yama.

'I believe you all have special skills to carry out this plot and more precise details will follow. Yama, you will take the shot, being ex-special forces and sniper trained. DuPlessis will handle logistics, supplies, and equipment. Rhazien, you will take out the CCTV, and Cassaire, you and your cohorts will handle the security guards. Any questions?'

'What about him?' said Yamauba, pointing at Maake.

'He will stay with me and keep me safe, then help me make sure the good doctor is dead,' Mogwai replied.

'Sounds like you've got it all worked out boss,' said Maake.

'This plan has taken me months to finalise in detail. Do not let me down. Make your way to Nairobi and wait for further instructions.'

*****

Narok had been listening to Mogwai's threat and was taken aback by the callous words he had heard. His worst fears were realised.

He took off immediately to return to the Tamonten Tusks to inform them their destiny was now clear.

They needed to save the doctor from the assassination attempt and allow him to speak against the criminals who wanted him out of the picture.

17

The Assassination

Summit to do with challenges and solutions

The day of the United Nations Environment Programme Summit had arrived and the city of Nairobi was bustling with activity. Most of the hotels were fully booked with delegates, tourists, and business people, making the most of East Africa's capital.

Nairobi had grown and continued to develop since the days when it was a relatively small British rail depot, and offered the visitor numerous things to do, including visiting parks, art museums, and cultural attractions.

As with most major cities, there were wealthy areas and poor areas, the Lanj'ata being the most sought after, and the Kibera being one of the poorest, where crime was a serious issue.

***

The Tamonten Tusks had made the long trek from their normal habitat in Tanzania to Kenya to attend the summit. Their mission was to try and protect Dr Max from the threat to his life Narok had discovered a few days before.

Mogwai's plans were unknown, but they knew that thwarting an assassination attempt on Dr Max was their destiny and they needed to be alert and on their guard. Narok had provided some intel on Mogwai's henchmen, so the four elephants needed to be vigilant and keep their eyes open for anything suspicious.

Two of them would be positioned near the entrance where delegates would have their passes scanned. From there, they would be able to observe everyone who went inside.

The other two would take up positions inside the building.

The conference centre entrance was closely guarded and consisted of a paved area, with four visitor corridors; steel balustrades separated each admission point.

At the end of the queuing areas there were two muscular uniformed rhino officers, with biceps bursting out of their tight shirts, holding devices to scan the barcodes on each delegate's lanyard.

It was 9.30 a.m. The conference was due to start at ten.

Visitors were now starting to arrive and assemble at the entrance in considerable numbers.

With security passes arranged by Dr Max, Kintaro and Yuki guarded the entrance to the scanning areas from either side and were looking out for anyone or anything suspicious.

Bosh had made his way to the front of the security

area where bags and briefcases would be searched. He climbed onto a kiosk containing spare lanyards. From there, he would be able to see what belongings visitors brought into the atrium area of the building.

Delegates assembled in the atrium, which had a huge skylight in the ceiling, allowing plenty of natural daylight. This area was perfect for everyone to catch up and network with acquaintances.

Bosh saw many different types of delegates, including representatives from neighbouring countries. There was an orangutan from Borneo draped in traditional dress, giraffes and zebra in business attire, farmers, kangaroos from Australia, and mandrill politicians, to name but a few.

The importance and significance of the event now dawned on him.

He did, however, notice some delegates he recognised, such as Monar the farmer, who had special dispensation to bring in some of his bees for his presentation, complete with a smoker to keep them calm.

Kingsley the park ranger was carrying a young black mamba snake, called Morris, in a cage.

Bosh also recognised Professor Gon, to whom he had not yet been introduced, but assumed it was him because he was the only fox there; he was wearing a monocle and had a black rhino as a companion.

As for Nakano, her task was to check out the conference room and look out for anything untoward.

***

The conference room was set up with herringbone-style seating.

There were approximately two hundred seats with a large stage at the front, and two presenter podiums both sides. In the middle of the stage was a table with microphones and four leather upholstered chairs.

At the back of the stage, mounted on the wall, was the blue and white emblem of the United Nations. It depicted the world and its waters wrapped in a wreath of olive branches.

On either side of the UN emblem were two huge TV screens, angled to face the left and right sides of the audience, so that conference speakers could be easily seen.

Nakano, along with other members of the security team, swept the seating area for any suspicious packages similar to the way a line of police officers search for clues.

All four were satisfied that security was tight and that they would be well-positioned should the conference be compromised.

**

Sometime earlier Mogwai's henchmen had initiated their cunning plan.

The first part of the plan was for Cassaire and her henchenas to make their way into the grounds of the headquarters. Once there, they would locate the Portakabin used by the contract security company Warthog Protection Services SA.

This was not difficult; the company's logo and contact details were attached to the door.

'Now; listen to me,' said Cassaire to her crack team – Vossler, Zul, Drach, Tidas, and Mortas, who were assembled behind a couple of rubbish skips ten metres away from the cabin. 'You know the plan: we overpower the guards and take their uniforms and passes, which needs to be achieved with a minimum of fuss.'

'Okay, boss, got it, boss,' they replied simultaneously.

The six hyenas, led by Cassaire, made their way low to the ground as if stalking prey and reached the side window of the cabin. Cassaire slowly stood on her back legs to peer inside, where she could see six warthog guards dressed in uniforms, but with no firearms. They were sitting at a table, smoking and playing poker, with a small amount of cash in the middle of the table.

'Okay, gang, this is it. I will lead – follow me.'

Cassaire burst through the door, snarling, with saliva dripping from her mouth, followed by her equally terrifying pack members. Vossler kicked the door shut.

The guards were terrified and backed off to the rear of the room.

'Don't be afraid, gentlemen. Luckily for you, we have already eaten today,' said Cassaire.

'Please don't hurt us,' one of the limp-wristed warthogs begged, 'what do you want?'

'We want you to strip,' said Cassaire.

'Strip?' said another terrified guard.

'Yes, get 'em off, and quick.'

One by one, the guards obeyed her order and took off their uniforms.

'Kindly place your security passes onto the table and keep still.' said Drach, holding some wrist ties. He started to handcuff each guard, with their hands behind their backs.

Next, Mortas came forward with grey duct tape, which he and Tidas ripped with their teeth and used to cover each guard's mouth from ear to ear.

Zul nudged Cassaire and said, 'What was I supposed to do, boss?'

'Just look menacing, you idiot,' said Cassaire.

The five bumbling hyenas put on the guards' uniforms and placed the security passes around their necks as Cassaire stood guard and snarled at the warthogs, who were now unable to move or speak.

'Thank you, gentlemen, you have been most cooperative,' she said.

She quickly donned her uniform and the six of them left the cabin, locking the door behind them.

First part of the plan completed, Cassaire thought, rather pleased with herself. The pack entered the main building.

***

Duplessis, apart from being an expert animal hustler, was also a master of obtaining the unobtainable. A sort of fixer, he could get you anything you wanted, but at a price.

Hence, he was the man to get Yamauba into the building, source a Barret self-assembly sniper rifle, and arrange extraction transport for a quick getaway.

In addition to transportation and firepower, the Dup also sourced a lighting technician's uniform and equipment. This would disguise Yama so he could enter the building as part of the technical team with a pass verifying his role.

Yama got dressed in the Dups van, parked a few hundred metres away from the building. He arranged his large heavy-duty holdall, which had a compartment at the bottom for his rifle, added some grenades, then covered them with cables, lamps, and tools, completing the impersonation of a lighting specialist. He slid open the side door of the van and casually walked across the road to the entrance to the UN building.

Just as he was about to join the queue, he spotted Kintaro supervising the delegates arriving. He doubled back for fear of being spotted by the seven-ton bouncer.

'Damn those Tusks,' he said to himself. 'How am I going to get past him without being spotted?'

Just then, the Dup arrived and tapped him on the shoulder. 'You forgot this, my friend.' He handed him the lighting company cap and an industrial face mask.

'Thanks a lot, Dup, I was beginning to panic, trying to get past that fat elephant.'

'No problem,' said the Dup, 'and good luck in there.'

Yama attempted his entry a second time, with head and face mostly covered, and only a cursory glance from Kintaro.

Once inside, Yama made his way to the atrium past

some chatting delegates, then through the double doors at the far end and into the main conference hall.

Once inside, he noticed final arrangements being made – sound checks on microphones.

'One, two … one two …' echoed around the room as hard copy agendas were placed on every delegate's seat.

This was a perfect opportunity for Yamauba to go unchallenged and find a position high enough, with a clear view of the two podiums on the stage.

He slipped through a no-entry door at the rear of the room and climbed some ladders to the fly and rigging system in the roof area, which extended the full length of the room to the stage.

In among all the ropes, booms, lifts, and hoists, he found a temporary suspension structure, normally used to support lighting equipment, and decided that this was the spot from which he could get a clear shot at Dr Max.

He placed his holdall on the structure in front of him and emptied the contents, removing the rifle parts from the foam cut-outs.

Once the rifle was assembled, he laid it on the platform, supported by barrel legs, and fitted the sight and silencer, ready to fire. Yamauba lay down by its side, waiting for the good doctor's speech to commence.

'In position,' he murmured to himself.

***

Nakano, having helped with the security arrangements in the main conference hall, rejoined Yuki and Kintaro in the atrium. Issun was now back on Kintaro's head.

'Has anyone seen Narok?' asked Kintaro. The others hadn't.

'Well I'm sure he will put in an appearance at some point.'

'Let's take our seats, everyone,' said Yuki, 'the conference is due to start any minute now.'

They took their allocated seats in the middle of the front row and Kintaro checked his agenda as to when Dr Max was scheduled to speak.

Quiet descended upon the audience when Nigerian Archbishop Alfred Adebayo entered the stage, followed by Maasai Chief Archer Saitoti, San Bushman leader, Arnold Dronin from Botswana, and Montgomerie 'Monty' the orangutan from Borneo.

Nakano's face lit up at the sight of her friend again, from her time in Thailand.

'It's Monty!' she whispered to Yuki. Kintaro shushed her.

The archbishop opened the conference, which took a while, as he had an unfortunate stammer, but he quickly regained the audience's attention with his well-rehearsed joke about visiting the doctor back home in Nigeria.

The joke was that when he visited his doctor complaining that he struggled to say the letters F and T, the doctor replied, 'Well, you can't say fairer than that!'

Nakano, still excited at the sight of Monty again, looked around her fellow delegates and to her horror saw Maake sitting next to a Chinese-looking man on the second row. She instantly knew it was Maake from the branding iron symbol 'Dare to be King' on his right hind leg.

How in god's name did they manage to get through security? she thought.

She also recognised Rhazien, two rows behind Maake, and instantly realised they must be up to something. She nudged Yuki and whispered her observations in her ear, mentioning that the sinister-looking Chinese man could also be up to no good.

'Keep your eyes on them, Nakano,' said Yuki, who in turn passed on the information to Kintaro.

Bosh, feeling as though he was being kept out of the loop, jabbed Kintaro on his head, demanding to know what was going on.

'Ouch,' winced the big guy, then updated Bosh for fear of being stabbed a second time.

Having finished his introduction, the archbishop announced the next guest speaker, who was Roman Esposito from Italy, talking about climate change.

'When is Dr Max due to speak?' Nakano asked.

'He's the third speaker. Amber Simmons after Roman, then it's the doctor,' Kintaro replied.

Roman's speech lasted about an hour, the conclusion being that the planet needed cooperation from China, the USA, and Russia if it was to stand any chance of reducing carbon emissions. Rapturous applause followed Mr Esposito's speech and the camera operators focused their lenses on the audience to film their reaction, the results projected onto the two large screens above the stage.

Next to speak was Amber Simmons from the USA, who looked a little awkward, given that her homeland was one of the three worst-performing nations in combating climate change.

Amber, an Alaskan lynx, was more concerned at this point about suppressing her nerves – she was scheduled to speak for thirty minutes. Her speech was promoting the Clean Seas Campaign, but once she got into her stride, the passion came through in abundance, especially relating to single-use plastics and changing mindsets.

'Wow, that was impressive,' said Dr Max, waiting in the wings at the end of Amber's speech. 'Follow that!'

No sooner had Amber left the stage, to yet more rapturous applause, than the archbishop introduced Dr Max. 'Can I have your attention, please? I would like to take a minute to introduce our next guest speaker. We have before us today a brilliant man, a self-made successful businessman, who has dedicated his wealth and the rest of his life to combating the illegal trade in ivory and to the conservation of endangered species. Please give a very warm welcome to Doctor Maximilian Schwarz.'

'Stay alert, everyone,' said Kintaro.

Almost time, Yama thought, *I'll let the audience finish their applause and allow the doctor to start his speech. Then I'll take the shot. It will be over in a second.*

'Not long now, Maake,' said Mogwai, 'we will be rid of the German do-gooder once and for all.'

As the tension built in anticipation of the doctor's

speech, a large bird swooped into the room.

'Look,' said Bosh, 'it's Narok.'

Narok was gliding from one side of the hall to the other.

'He did make it after all,' said Yuki.

Dr Max thanked the audience for their kind welcome and began his speech. 'I would like to talk to you today about life on land, its challenges and solutions …'

'Any second now,' Yama said to himself as he manoeuvred his rifle to face the left side of the podium.

Narok, with his all-seeing eyes, caught a glimpse of the assassin high up on the rigging platform and identified him as Yamauba, readying himself to take the shot.

He swooped down and picked out Kintaro and Issun on the front row. 'Yama's about to shoot,' he said.

Issun instantly leapt off Kintaro's head and onto his feet. He ran to the stage and positioned himself in front of the doctor's podium, slamming his ivory needle into the stage beneath him.

At that precise moment, Yamauba pulled the trigger. The bullet hit the now full-grown Issun Boshi in the chest instead of its intended target. Shock and chaos ensued as Issun's lifeless body hit the wooden stage with a thud. Panic erupted among the audience and the doctor didn't know which way to turn.

Yama, realising that his shot had missed the doctor and hit Issun instead, reached for a hand grenade from his holdall and launched it at the stage.

'Grenade!' Nakano shouted as she spotted the

incendiary device hurtling its way towards the dignitaries on the stage. She focused on the falling bomb and somehow managed to divert it away from the stage and towards the sound system station to its right. The two technicians fled for their lives just before the grenade exploded.

Seconds later, Cassaire and her henchmen, dressed as security guards, appeared from nowhere and ushered Dr Max away from the podium and down some steps to so-called safety.

***

'Damn those elephants!' Yama cursed as he realised his attempt had failed. He promptly dismantled the rifle and returned it to his holdall. 'Got to get out of here,' he murmured to himself and climbed down from the elevated platform and onto the ladder to make his escape.

Monar the farmer could not believe what was happening. He kept his eyes on the doctor who had been so good to him and watched him being led down the steps into the now half-empty room.

This does not look right, he thought as the suspicious-looking hyenas in ill-fitting uniforms forcibly led the doctor towards him.

'Stop, stop right there!' he shouted.

'Get out of my way, peasant.' Cassaire snarled.

Monar released the bees and set them loose upon the bogus guards, causing a state of frenzy and forcing them to release their prisoner.

Dr Max ran towards Monar and they looked to escape while a saloon brawl ensued between the bees and dogs. It was another stand-off and one the bees were looking forward to.

Fabio and his Mafioso bees hovered in a line against six snarling striped hyenas, also positioned in a line.

One of the bees spoke out. 'So, you bring me this on the day of my daughter's wedding?' Fabio had always wanted to say that line.

'Shut up, flea,' Cassaire replied.

'Mama Mia,' Enzo replied, 'so, you think, you're a tough girl, hey?'

'You do frighten us,' said Mortas, the scaredy-cat.

'Quiet, weakling,' said Vossler. 'We can take them – they're only bees and we're ferocious hyenas.' He was trying to convince himself.

'So, you want a rumble in the jungle, hey?' said Toni, joining in the fight.

'Bring it on,' said Drach, laughing uncontrollably.

'Remind me why are we here,' Zul said, forgetting everything.

Angelo replied, 'It's a sting and you are about to get stung pooch!'

Profanities exchanged, the two sides entered into combat, buzzing, screaming, kicking, arms waving, stings administered, and hyenas fighting each other in the confusion.

No prizes for guessing who the first to retreat were and it wasn't the honey-producing marvels.

***

Monar's chaperoning of Dr Max did not last long; as they entered the atrium they were greeted by Mogwai and Maake.

'We'll take him from here, peasant farmer,' said Mogwai.

Maake wasted no time in slapping the brave farmer on the nose and knocking him unconscious.

The doctor finally realised that he was being abducted and he felt a sharp metallic object digging into his waist as Mogwai manhandled him.

'No sudden moves, Doctor … I have a knife,' said Mogwai.

The two men and Maake made their way out of the building, into the bustling Village Market mall nearby, and blended in amongst the crowds.

However, after helping casualties in the main building, Kintaro spotted Maake, Mogwai, and the doctor and gave chase.

Yuki's only concern was for Issun Boshi, motionless on the stage. 'Issun,' she shouted. As she was making her way to the stage she was confronted by Duplessis, who threw a weighted net over her, causing her to fall.

Her instinct was to become invisible, but it was futile; the netting would not have allowed her to escape.

'Sorry, my dear, but I can get top rand for you in Asia,' the Dup said.

'Leave her alone,' said a voice from behind the Dup. 'You mess with my friends, you mess with me.'

'Go away, monkey,' DuPlessis replied.

'I'm an orangutan,' Monty corrected.

Nakano's friend administered several martial art blows to the Dup, rendering him unconscious.

'Let me help you, my dear,' said Monty, removing the net.

Nakano arrived on the scene and helped Monty free Yuki.

'Thank you both. I'm okay, but what about poor Bosh?' she said.

However, her tangle with the Dup was not the last of it. Rhazien appeared at the foot of the steps.

'What about poor Bosh? Is he alive or is he dead?' said the spotted hyena, pacing to the right and the left.

'Get out of the way, Rhazien!' said Nakano.

'Or what?' the laughing hyena replied.

'You'll see.'

Nakano and Monty flew at Rhazien, and a vicious fight ensued.

***

Professor Gon and Clem had made their way out of the main hall and into the atrium.

Having seen Dr Max escorted to apparent safety by Mogwai and Maake, they wanted to be sure for themselves that he was okay.

'My dear Clem, what on earth just happened in there? I heard gunshots, explosions and saw bees fighting with hyenas. Not to mention a poor elephant shot and another suffer an attempted kidnapping! In all the years I have been attending these conferences, I have never seen anything like the events at this one.'

'Maybe they should be a bit more careful who they invite next time,' said Clem.

'Do you know, old chap, I think you're right. We seem to have been in amongst all kinds of riff-raff. Standards are not what they used to be.'

The two friends left the building and went into the grounds, hoping to catch up with the doctor and make sure he was in good hands.

'That lion with the doc looked a bit shifty to me,' said Clem.

'I agree, Clem, and I thought the same about the Chinese gentleman too,' Gon replied.

As they passed some of the outside portakabins, the professor noticed a warthog, gagged and headbutting the window inside one of the cabins.

'Look, Clem,' Gon said, 'that gent looks locked in against his will. Do something, Clem.'

Clem didn't need an invitation and charged the door on the right-hand side of the cabin, completely obliterating at least a third of the structure as if it had been split by a giant chainsaw. All that remained of the cabin was three side walls, half a roof, and six semi-naked warthogs, bound and gagged.

The professor entered what was left of the cabin and freed the security warthogs, while Clem removed bits of plasterboard and rubble from his horn.

'Gentlemen, you must help us – we fear a very important person is in danger!' said Gon.

The warthogs agreed to help and joined Gon and Clem in giving chase, albeit in their underpants.

***

Kintaro had almost caught up with the villains as they were about to enter the Village Market mall next door to the UN headquarters.

Mogwai sensed that they were being followed and turned around to see Kintaro's enormous frame with tusks like torpedoes and a trunk the size of a sampan cabin. 'Deal with him, Maake, and meet us later at the extraction point,' he ordered.

Maake stopped and waited for his adversary in the foyer of the shopping mall.

Kintaro entered the mall and stopped about four metres away from the fearsome lion, who bore the Dare to be King symbol like a medal of bravery. He stood motionless, showing an intimidating display of his impressive teeth. He had four seven-centimetre canines either side of his incisors and front teeth specifically designed for tearing meat.

After letting out a threatening growl, he addressed the big K. 'I said that our paths would cross again, didn't I? Well, you're going to need that extra strength the vulture gave you.'

'Do you think so, pussy cat?' Kintaro replied.

Maake started to circle Kintaro, weighing up his

options. The mall's shoppers cleared the area fearing that something unpleasant was about to happen.

Kintaro watched Maake's every move, knowing that the slightest lapse in concentration could be fatal.

'So, this will decide the true King of the Savannas,' said Maake.

Kintaro was quick to respond 'They say that being runner-up is worthless, but you will soon have to get used to it.'

That was the final insult for Maake and he leapt at the big K, administering a right hook to the side of the elephant's head, which instantly put Kintaro on the deck.

Kintaro hit the ground with such force that it cracked the tiled floor beneath him. No sooner had he shook his head than Maake was on his back, claws drawing blood from Kintaro's shoulders and sinking his huge teeth into his left ear.

Kintaro let out a trumpeting cry of pain and sprang to his feet, the lion still attached. Unable to shake him off, he charged at one of the shops and burst through the window, glass shattering everywhere.

Maake had no other choice but to release Kintaro, and suffered glass cuts to his face and legs. With shards of glass still implanted in his body, Maake readied himself for another onslaught, growling as if to let Kintaro know that he wasn't hurt.

Kintaro, however, was relieved that he had shaken off the street-fighting lion and took a moment to consider his next option. *I have to defeat Maake by defending myself,* he thought, and prepared himself to allow the lion another attack.

Maake obliged and thrust himself at Kintaro's front, hoping to get at the elephant's eyes.

Big mistake. Kintaro's tusks flipped Maake up and over his head and the big cat landed on his back.

That must have hurt, thought Kintaro, but the defiant lion got straight up and circled him once more.

Kintaro edged his way backwards and out of the shop, back into the mall, giving Maake the impression that he was tiring and showing signs of weakness.

The lion followed Kintaro out of the shop, believing that the elephant would not be able to withstand another onslaught.

He once again leapt at his opponent, but Kintaro was too quick and grabbed Maake by the throat, slamming him onto the floor. The big K dived on top of the cat rendering him unable to breathe let alone move.

Maake was reeling from Kintaro's sheer weight and squealed in pain. 'Okay, okay, you win. I surrender, Kintaro, get off me!'

Kintaro obliged and the defeated, badly hurt lion limped off with his tail between his legs.

***

Mogwai had not made much progress with Dr Max. Trying to force a six-foot hostage in a certain direction wasn't easy when the abductor was a foot shorter and considerably weaker. The threat of the knife, however, was enough to ensure the doctor complied with Mogwai's demands.

They had made their way outside the mall and into the recreation ground, where Mogwai was expecting to see Duplessis with transport to make their getaway.

Kintaro had no idea where Mogwai was, having had to deal with Maake, but knew that he would not stay in the shopping mall and probably had transport lined up to collect them. He took an emergency exit and found himself in the grounds of the mall, but there was still no sign of Mogwai.

Give me something, Narok. Where are you when I need you? he thought.

As if by divine intervention, Narok appeared in the sky, hovering over a specific area.

That must be where the doctor is ... Narok is showing me where they are.

He quickly followed the eagle's lead and charged through an open gate into the recreation area. Mogwai and the doctor were now in Kintaro's sights and waiting where they were probably expecting to rendezvous for a speedy getaway.

'Where the hell is Dup?' said Mogwai.

The Dup could not make it with the transport; Monty and Nakano had seen to that.

As Kintaro approached Mogwai, he saw the professor, Clem, and six warthogs in their underpants moving in on them. Next to arrive at the scene were Kingsley and the caged mamba accompanied by Monar at Mogwai's rear.

He was surrounded and twisted and turned to confirm how outnumbered he was.

'Get back, or the doc gets it,' said Mogwai, his knife penetrating the doctor's skin almost to the point of drawing blood.

'It's over, Mogwai, give yourself up,' said Kingsley, who had released Morris the mamba, before Mogwai realised who had spoken.

'Never,' Mogwai replied and, realising his fate, gestured as if to thrust the knife into the doctor's chest. At that moment, the snake bit Mogwai on his calf and he dropped the knife instantly.

Kingsley and Monar pounced and apprehended Mogwai, who was reduced to his knees.

'Better get him to the hospital before the venom kicks in,' said Kingsley.

'How did you get a pet mamba?' Kintaro asked.

'He was injured when Nakano used him to scare away the poachers when we were attacked and I have cared for him ever since,' Kingsley replied.

'He will go down in hissstory,' said Clem getting no reaction from his fellow rescuers.

Dr Max thanked everyone for rescuing him but reminded them that there had been a shooting and a brave elephant had taken the bullet meant for himself. He suggested they returned immediately.

***

Back at the UN headquarters, they encountered the

aftermath of the assassination attempt. Police were everywhere and paramedics were attending to multiple bee stings on Cassaire and her pack.

Kintaro ran towards Nakano and Yuki, who were being consoled by Monty.

'How is Bosh?' he asked, fearing the worst.

'He's gone,' Nakano replied.

Kintaro slumped to his knees in grief.

'I'm so sorry, everyone,' said Doctor Max, 'he gave up his life to protect me.'

'My condolences, ladies,' added the professor.

'No, you don't understand, *he's gone*!' said Yuki.

'Gone where?' Kintaro asked.

'We have looked everywhere for him. There was no trail of blood to guide us … we checked the stage, the seating, the atrium, everywhere.'

'I have spoken with the authorities and nothing has been reported,' said Nakano.

'We hoped that maybe Issun had morphed back to his miniature state and attempted to find us.'

'There has to be a body, tiny as it may be, but I cannot believe that he has disappeared,' said Kintaro, 'we have to keep looking.'

'Where is Narok when you need him most?' said Yuki.

Everyone was dumbfounded, apart from Narok, the martial eagle with the all-seeing eye…

Printed in Great Britain
by Amazon